Down The Cannon

Gerald D. Otis

Down The Cannon is a fictional story based on a mix of fictional and real characters and fictional and real events. Dialogue, characterizations and incidents involving locally well-known historical figures are products of the author's imagination and are not to be construed as real. They are not intended to depict actual events or people or to change the fictional nature of the work. In all other respects, any resemblance to actual persons, living or dead, events, or locales is entirely coincidental.

Cover Photo by: Jim Berhow

Printed in the United States of America

This novel is dedicated to the current and former citizens of Northfield, Minnesota, the author's home town. Growing up in Northfield in the 1950s and 1960s and driving taxi cab there produced indelible adventures and experiences , many of which remain vivid some 65 years later. The characters that populated this small town ran the gamut from erudite professors to uneducated school drop-outs; from skilled artisans in nearly every field of endeavor to those who bumbled along living by their wits; from those who were warm, friendly and caring to those who were coarse, hostile and belligerent; from military veterans to those who served in other ways; from the guardians of civic values to irresponsible drunkards. Thank you all for helping me to understand and appreciate the many different ways of being in the world.

CONTENTS

ACKNOWLEDGMENTS

The author wishes to thank his dear friend, Jim Berhow, for reading early chapters of this book and reminding him of people and incidents that he had forgotten or overlooked. Jim also deserves credit for the photograph of the State Bank and Cannon River used on the cover of this book. A special thank you to Dolly Roush and her keen eye for catching numerous errors in an earlier version of the manuscript. B. Wayne Quist compiled the letters of Lars Kindem into the very readable memoir *Dear Donald* (ISBN: 978-1505250022), which jogged my memory of many names, places, and events. Another historian of Northfield memorabilia in the 1950s who stimulated some long-dormant memory neurons was Terry DeWolfe, who graduated from NHS a few years before me. And I would be amiss if I didn't mention Maggie Lee's book, *Northfield Ink* (ISBN: 0-9707020-9-4), and her many columns about local personalities in the *Northfield News*. Special thanks go to John R. Graham, Michael Napoliello, and Lynda Southworth (my favorite schoolmarm and Playboy

Bunny) for reading and providing comments that improved the quality of the book. Finally, I would like to thank my wife Connie for putting up with my endless hours at the computer instead of fixing all the broken-down possessions that we accumulated over the years.

For those readers who are sticklers for historical accuracy, please excuse my exercise of dramatic license to change some timelines and events to fit the fictional story herein presented.

1 THE GANG

Milt gazed out the large front window of the Crow's Nest bar at the building across the street – the State Bank of Northfield. It was a beautiful semi-circular cream-colored structure of Egyptian Revival design situated on a pie-shaped lot on the western bank of the Cannon River. The twin bronze-plated front doors were framed by two parallelogram columns, wider at the base than at the top, and the structure was crowned with a circular green-hued glass dome.

"H'm," said Milt to himself as he absent-mindedly wiped the gleaming mahogany bar with his towel. "I wonder when they built that place?"

Desiree Goodlove sidled up to a position opposite Milt at the bar. "Penny for your thoughts, Milty," she said.

"Slow night, eh Des?" countered Milt.

Des was the kind of girl that was popular with all the androgen-infused young men in town, particularly with those who wanted a sexual encounter at a fair price with no commitment to a longer relationship. It was rumored that she once pleasured nearly the whole high school basketball team one night on the hood of a hearse parked in Fat Freddy Ferguson's back yard. This night she was dressed invitingly with frayed denim short-shorts and breasts spilling out of the man's long sleeve shirt she wore with tails tied at the waist and buttons open almost to the navel. She had a thin jaw and a wiry body that she could move with ease in a sultry way, not exactly a classic beauty but attractive enough to draw the attention of the young studs that were her prey.

"Yeah, guess all the guys are at the ball game or home with their disgruntled wives. Maybe they'll show up later. A girl's gotta make her rent, ya know."

Milt had more than one fling with Des and she never failed to please. He liked Des's provocativeness and devil-may-care attitude. She hadn't had many breaks in life and he tried to help her out when he could.

"Have a beer on me, Des. Take up a seat in that second booth from the end where you can see the TV. Cross your legs – show your gams. Someone will come along sooner or later."

"You look after me just like a daddy should," said Des as she sashayed down the floor.

Milt saw Howard Kinlaw enter the bar and, smiling, made eye contact with him as he took up a stool at the counter. "How goes it, Howard? Want a draft?"

"Yeah, that sounds good," Howard responded. "Been a long day fixing shit those fucking students broke."

Milt poured the draft and slid it in front of Howard. "That'll be 15 cents," he said. Howard reached into his pants pocket and pulled out the change.

Howard was a maintenance man at Carleton College, the institution where he had previously been a student majoring in physics. He dropped out in his junior year when his girlfriend was unfaithful to him with his best friend. There followed a period of depression, quick affairs, drinking, and carousing.

Howard developed a lot of resentment for having been betrayed and found it hard to trust others ever since. He struck up an acquaintance with Milt in the course of frequenting this tavern where Milt acted as his bartender-therapist while Howard disgorged his maudlin tales of woe as he descended into a drunken stupor. Milt enjoyed playing the role mainly because it didn't cost him much and it put him in a position where he could ask favors and exert some control over his patron. Howard, normally quiet and socially shy, appreciated Milt's sympathetic ear and willingness to take him into his fold.

"You up for tonight?" Milt asked.

Peering up from his beer, Howard glimpsed Milt's crooked grin set in a face of chiseled features and quickly returned to inspecting the bubbles rising in his beer.

"Reckon so," replied Howard. "I need a challenge to pick me up and get me out of this goddamn funk." He smiled to himself as he recalled how his mind was totally focused, his heart was pumping with anticipation, and his actions and reactions were perfectly coordinated the last time he went on one of these adventures with Milt.

"That's the ticket," said Milt. "Start the ball rolling! Then come back and let Des lift your spirits for a spell. She has a knack for it, ya know?"

"Yeah, I know," said Howard, a sly grin gracing his face.

Howard finished his beer, glanced around the room to see if anyone had been eavesdropping on his conversation with Milt, then got off the stool and made his way to the door, tossing off a "See ya Milt!" as he departed.

Once outside, Howard made a beeline for the Flying A gas station next door at the base of the five-story Malt-O'Meal plant, the former Ames Mill. Clarence Dixon was washing the windshield of a car while waiting for its gas tank to fill from a gas pump with a round glass bulb on top displaying the winged 'A' logo for Tidewater Associated Oil Company, also known as Tydol or Veedol depending upon who owned the company at the time. Once the car left and no one was waiting, Clarence came over to talk with Howard. "Let's go over on the bridge so I can have a cigarette, said Clarence. "Mr. Stark gets mad every time I blow up the place."

"I reckon he would," Howard guffawed.

The pair made their way the few yards over to the cement bridge on Fourth Street where they could watch the river flowing over the dam or watch the traffic coming over the bridge from either direction. Each lit a cigarette and looked at the water cascading over the dam, hemmed in on one side by the basement of the Malt-O'Meal Plant and on the other by a two-story cement wall with an 18-inch walkway just above the waterline and topped by a black five foot wrought iron railing meant to prevent fishermen and gawkers from falling into the river. Large brown and yellow carp were swimming next to the sewer drain outlet in the corner bounded by the dam and the wall.

"Milt says it's on for tonight. Do you want to tell Dale? I'll go over and tell Billy."

"Okey-dokey," said Clarence. "Boy, that Milt is quite the guy, huh? Keeps us entertained and gives us a little pocket change too."

Howard glanced at Clarence with a questioning expression on his face, but said only, "Yeah. He's quite a guy alright."

Clarence was tall and muscular with a healthy crop of blond hair topped by a sweat-stained short-visored cap. He grew up on a farm south of town. His father had to warn him, after a few regrettable incidents, to be careful in the use of his size and strength so that he didn't inadvertently hurt small animals and other kids. Thus, Clarence tended to approach others in a kind, gentle and considerate manner. But he knew how others perceived him and used it to his advantage when needed. And he could explode with violence or mean vindictiveness at times.

Clarence did OK in school when it involved memorizing facts and doing routine arithmetical calculations but he had difficulty as he encountered more abstract and fuzzy concepts. As his limitations became more evident, he suffered from being labeled a "dumb farm kid" and he became more sensitive to slights as former friends chose to distance themselves from him. He usually had only one or two friends and feared losing them but he found that he could ensure their respect and loyalty by beating up their enemies, being overly forgiving of their foibles, and flattering them with praise whether they deserved it or not.

His choice of friends suffered from a lack of discernment of character and he would at times be betrayed by someone he idealized, causing him to simultaneously want to beat the betrayer to a pulp while at the same time feeling he should follow his father's instruction, check his anger and give him another chance.

Clarence met Milt in high school and they both were on the wrestling team and would go hunting and fishing together. Milt had a swagger and self-confidence that Clarence admired and he tended to idealize him. Milt liked having some "muscle" around when he would antagonize others and knew that Clarence thrived on the friendship and regard shown to him. Nevertheless, Milt couldn't restrain himself, at times, from making fun of Clarence's limitations in front of others. If he saw that he had gone over the line in hurting Clarence's feelings, however, he would quickly grab him around the shoulders and claim that he was just engaging in lighthearted ribbing. Clarence would be relieved and easily go into a forgiving mode, even though he did not completely believe it.

Howard finished his cigarette and flipped it into the swirling currents below. "I've got to get going. Have to let Billy know. You need to tell Dale the next time he comes around."

"OK. You can take that to the bank. See you tonight"

Howard walked to the other side of the bridge then continued north, peering into the windows of the State Bank and Anderson's Furniture Store as he passed. He stopped at Hughes and Heckler Hardware to check out the Smith & Wesson automatic in the widow display then proceeded a few more steps to Friggi's Cafe. Taking a seat at the empty short lunch counter, he was greeted by Billy Griffin when he came to wait on him. "Hi, Howard. What'll it be?"

"Oh, just a cup of coffee and one of those plain crusty donuts," said Howard.

Billy brought the coffee and donut and lingered in front of Howard, trying to act nonchalant and give the impression he was just shooting the breeze with a customer. Billy was the kind of guy that ordinarily was enthusiastic about everything - people, food, clothes, animals, the natural world. He liked to live a carefree life and didn't let any rules of decorum interfere with his sensual pleasure-seeking. In his teen years, Billy's desire for a feckless lifestyle was held in check by a domineering and over-controlling stepfather who didn't spare the rod.

Billy had one outstanding talent – a gift for almost photo-realistic drawing that impressed most people who viewed his work. He could draw an object, an animal, a person and capture that movement that made them unique. At a different time and place, with a different set of parents, that faculty might have been encouraged in productive directions. As it was, Billy used it to impress girls and draw caricatures for small sums of money.

Howard played along with the casual conversation ruse and then asked in a soft voice, "The thing is on for tonight. Can you make it?"

"I'll be there. Have to work at 3D Friday night." Then he quickly moved away, pretending to have to tend to something in the kitchen.

Howard noted the uncharacteristic awkwardness in Billy's manner and assumed it was his previously expressed apprehension about the enterprise that engaged them. Billy was a party animal, taking people at face value and ignoring hidden implications in their words and deeds. People liked Billy and envied his carefree enjoyment of the sensual life. But Howard knew that any situation that required looking into the future and making a commitment made Billy anxious. He once confessed to Howard, "I panic when I feel pinned down or trapped because I 'have to' do something. I dread the thought of not having any options if I don't like the feel of things."

Howard worried that Billy didn't think ahead and plan for different contingencies and that could spell danger for everyone. He pondered the matter as he finished his coffee, paid his tab, and headed for home.

***

Dale Halverson dropped off a passenger at Milt's bar in his black 1954 Chevrolet Bel Air sedan with the white plastic "Taxi" sign on top and lingered in front, slowly recording his last fare and counting his change, waiting to see if Milt would come out to notify him of any new plans.

Dale grew up the son of a machinist who worked at the Northfield Foundry putting wood-working machines together. The senior Halverson was a WWII vet who had seen a lot of combat in Europe and had exceeded the magic number of 25 missions bomber crews were expected to survive. Back from the war, he contained his chronic anxiety by compulsive activity in his photography hobby, such as meticulously removing all the hairs, one by one, in the negative of an unshaven man.

Dale's dad had to have everything exact and controlled: meals at the same time every day, furniture sparse and neatly arranged; outings to be well-planned days in advance; wife to introduce no surprises to his routine. Dale couldn't stand the regimentation and often acted out, doing daredevil things because they were exciting, impressed his peers, and freaked out his father. His mother begged him to let his father be and he usually did yet was baffled by his father's behavior. He had no idea what his father feared and had tried, in vain, to show his father there was nothing to be afraid of. Dale's sometimes reckless endeavors on occasion brought him into contact with the police and with school authorities who termed him "Dauntless Dale."

Dale liked individual sports like track, wrestling and gymnastics, and being instructed by a tough coach. He liked to challenge his endurance and would run until he was so exhausted that he developed cramps and was forced by accumulating lactic acid and failing muscles to stop. Dale knew both Milt and Clarence from high school and they often partied together, pulled pranks on others, and engaged in petty vandalism, like stealing a car to go joyriding or breaking into the grain elevator over on West Second Street, just to look around and prove they could do it.

Dale approached people and events as a dispassionate observer making him appear distant, aloof, and even arrogant at times. He liked objective analysis for its own sake and viewed criticism and disagreement as constructive rather than as a personal attack. He welcomed tough critiques that helped him achieve greater accuracy and objectivity. He sometimes inadvertently offended others by his objective criticism, which he did not see as a criticism of the person but of the idea they were expressing. To others, he seemed to be unfeeling and uninterested because he didn't want his personal feelings to distort his objectivity.

Milt came out the door of the bar with his apron in his hand, walked up to the passenger side door, and stuck his head in the window. Clarence started to walk over to Dale's cab from the Flying A but saw Milt heading for the car and returned to the station. "It's a go for tonight, said Milt. We meet at Tiny's about 7:00 and go from there."

"See ya then," said Dale as he put his cab in gear, made a U-turn at the Flying A, and drove down to the 1100 Taxi office next to the Riverside Cafe. Inside the office, Dale reported the amount of his fares to the dispatcher, "Pop" Jones.

Pop looked and talked a lot like Sidney Greenstreet in *The Maltese Falcon* except he had more slurring of his words. He was tall and fat and constrained his movements as much as possible while sitting in his oak swivel chair. He always had a Dutch Master cigar in his mouth, stained the color of tobacco, and he chewed and gyrated his cigar as he talked. From behind the dispatcher's desk Pop tapped, or more accurately, bounced his foot on the floor, the rate increasing as he became more agitated, either at one of the drivers or at some political point he was trying to make.

Pop was born on a farm in southern Minnesota

some 66 years earlier and married when he was young. He wanted to go to college but both parents died in the flu pandemic of 1918. He was spared participation in WWI because he was the sole person left to run the family farm, although he detested farming. He sold the farm he inherited from his father in the early 1920s and hired himself out as a "driver" for people in the illegal liquor industry during prohibition. He and Razzer Otis both worked for a woman bathtub gin manufacturer and were called upon to hide the consumables in snowbanks when alerted that the police were going to conduct raids. With the money he saved plus the proceeds from his farm sale, he bought a few cars and started a cab company of his own in 1934. Providing for his wife and three daughters kept him out of WWII and he made a lot of money during that turmoil since the principals in the other two cab companies in town were called to military service, so he had the whole taxi business in Northfield to himself.

Authoritarian, tough-minded, and domineering, Pop was referred to as "The Kingfish" by some. He always wanted to run a manufacturing company but had neither the education, nor talent for coming up with a competitive product. Nevertheless, he was good at organizing and keeping employees in line. He was overly protective of his daughters and longed for a son to carry on his legacy but fate would not have it. Consequently, he treated his younger male driver-employees as pseudo-sons, thus acquiring the nickname "Pop." He was angered by disrespect and anxious about losing anything that he had acquired. He now saw himself as a "respectable citizen" who had outrun his rum-runner past.

***

Tiny's Smoke Shop was the center of town for teenage and young adult males. Before "Professor Harold Hill" was able to warn about the "trouble" in "River City," Iowa, parents in this southern Minnesota town rallied to save their offspring from temptations of the flesh. Girls were warned by mothers and teachers to stay away from this squalid retreat for the foul-mouthed and unbathed denizens of the back streets of Northfield. But now and then a pair of girls would take up the dare and venture into this den of iniquity. They went in pairs for protection and usually left after a few minutes in a flurry of twitters about something they saw or heard.

What was all the fuss about? Well, Tiny's had everything a young stud wearing a black leather jacket and motorcycle boots with a duck's ass haircut would want: comic books, crotch novels, girly magazines, *Rod & Driver*, smokes of any kind, cherry cokes, hot dogs, prophylactics, candles, toothpaste, aviator sunglasses, model airplane kits, gizmos to make people laugh or change a dollar bill into $10 as if by magic. Tiny asserted that his business motto was, "If I don't have it, you don't need it."

And in the backroom – full-sized regulation pool tables! One billiards table with no pockets, two snooker tables, and one, near the back door overlooking the river, was for the game of Eight Ball. Along the north wall were pew-type benches for onlookers or those waiting in line, although some patrons used them to sleep on. Everyone smoked so various containers were available for ashes and spent cigarette butts. But, if those weren't convenient, there was always the floor. Some pool sharks tried to make a few dollars betting they could win and some onlookers created their own betting pools. Occasionally, a fight would break out when someone felt he had been duped or cheated but Tiny would quickly intervene, grabbing the offender (or both parties) by the ear lobe and marching them out the back door.

Stanley "Tiny" Johnson moved to Northfield in 1946 after running a restaurant in Renville and doing military construction during WWII. He was ironically dubbed "Tiny" by friends because of his huge size. He tolerated no loud swearing or roughhousing and closed the pool hall on Sundays so boys could attend church. Because of his stern but fair manner, he was credited with having kept more boys out of trouble than did the police. It was curious that, fifteen miles away in Farmington, there was another "Tiny" with similar personal characteristics, who ran a corner restaurant. He had essentially the same function with his youthful patrons as did the Northfield Tiny.

Tiny had a coterie of very devoted fans, among young men, who sent him cards and pictures when they married, had children, took a trip, or went off to war in Korea. When the city council proposed that some of the local "characters" not be allowed to sit in Riverside Park, Tiny carried a sign through the downtown area proclaiming "I am a Character!" and subsequently created the Characters Club in what used to be the barbershop below the Scriver Building on Bridge Square.

About seven o'clock, Milt and the gang descended on Tiny's and gathered at the Eight Ball table next to the back door. Milt and Clarence challenged Howard and Dale to a game of Eight Ball with Billy watching from his seat against the wall.

Milt won the coin toss and broke the rack of balls at the end of the table, managing to sink one ball in the process. As he took a bead on the One Ball, he said softly, "Oles or Carls?"

All the others cast their votes and Milt said "Oles it is." He took his shot and missed. "Damn! Clarence and me in front?" All agree. "Billy, you want to drive?"

"Sure," says Billy. "I'm parked over in front of the Ideal."

By the time the group finished their game, all the snooker tables were occupied and it was nearly dark. Two left by the back door and three exited the front with Tiny noting their departure by a fixed gaze at the backs of the departing customers. All gang members gathered at Billy's sleek blue and white 1950 Mercury Coupe. Clarence, occupying the most space, sat in the front passenger seat while the other three wedged themselves into the back seat.

"We're off," said Billy as he put the V-8 into gear and released the clutch. They made their way to St. Olaf Avenue and headed toward the college on a hill one mile to the west. "OK," said Milt. "We're looking for two or three students, maybe four, but no more than that, heading up the avenue. We want them to be separated from any other group by at least a block."

Soon they spotted a candidate group of three, a boy and two girls, near Plum Street and there was no one close to them on either side. Milt gave the order, "Drive up to Manitou and drop us off at the corner. Clarence and I will go up to Gensing Court and hide a bit back from the sidewalk. Park up the street away and when they go by the corner, Howard and Dale will come up behind. When it's over, we meet back at the car. Clarence and I will cut through the back yards over to Manitou. Be sure to wear your masks."

Taking their positions on Gensing Court, an unpaved single lane off St. Olaf Avenue nearly hidden from view by an overgrowth of trees and bushes, Milt and Clarence waited until they heard the sound of voices. Just before the jolly and unsuspecting students were about to pass, they jumped out and blocked the sidewalk. Startled and afraid, the students backed up and looked behind themselves to see two more masked men approaching. The girls shrieked and the boy moved ahead a little as if he might do battle to protect the girls.

"Good evening, friends," said Milt as he brandished his revolver and Clarence raised a club. "We won't hurt you or detain you long if you just cooperate and give us all your money. I'm sure you recognize it is hopeless to resist but if you choose to, you can expect to be missing a lot of school for the next few weeks."

The petrified girls looked at each other and began to fumble in their purses. The boy reached for his wallet.

"Here, gimme those," growled Clarence in as threatening a manner as he could muster. He threw one of the purses to the pair of muggers in the back and gave the wallet to Milt to pilfer.

"What have we here?" said Clarence as he found a secret compartment in the purse he was plundering. He quickly put the contents in his pocket along with the cash from the girl's billfold, tossing the purse on the ground when finished.

Milt yelled out, "Ready, boys? Let's hit it!" and they were all gone in a flash. The shaken students looked around toward Manitou and the desperadoes behind them had vanished also, the contents of their emptied purses and wallet strewn on the ground. The girls started to cry. The boy tried to comfort them and reassure them that the police would catch the culprits and retrieve their money.

Milt and Clarence sprinted to the lone house on Gensing Court and cut across backyards to the Gulbronsen House on Manitou where Billy was parked. Breathless, they jumped into the car already occupied by Howard and Dale. Billy sped off toward Greenvale Avenue, leaving his lights off until they crested the hill, then headed down to the wooden bridge over the railroad tracks and onto Highway 3 going south.

"Five minutes," said Dale, looking at his watch. "Pretty good time, I'd say."

"Holy shit," exclaimed Clarence as he pulled his loot out of his pocket. "That girl had $100 tucked away in her purse beside the $20 she had in her billfold."

"I got $35 out of the other purse," said Dale.

"The guy only had $23 in his wallet," said Milt.

"So we made about $35 apiece," said Howard. "Not great but not bad for five minutes work – a lot better than minimum wage."

"My hands are still shaking," said Billy. "I was scared shitless that Tasty Robinson would come along in the squad car before we got out of there."

"Take it easy, Billy," said Milt as he touched the driver's shoulder. "We don't want any busy-bodies taking note of this car. It's conspicuous enough as it is. We want to be unobtrusive everyday motorists. Just drive under the speed limit 'til we get where we're going." Billy kept it down to 25 mph until he got past Hughe's Market on Water Street then veered right on Highway 3 and matched the speed limit for the three miles to the village of Dundas.

Spirits were high as the gang settled into a booth at the Corner Bar. Patrons were getting pretty noisy which made conversation difficult but obscured the discourse between members so that eavesdroppers would have a hard time discerning what they were about. Howard, the analyst, believed that the "confronters" adequately scared the victims into submission. Dale thought the participants could have shaved off a few seconds of contact time by grabbing the money containers immediately without having a polite discourse about robbing the marks. Billy couldn't think of anything that would have made him more unfazed – he just thought of all the ways things could go wrong.

Clarence grunted and said, "We scared the crap out of them. They won't remember a thing."

Milt thought things went pretty well, that everyone followed orders and played their parts as they were directed. "Maybe we are ready for something more challenging."

2 TAXI! TAXI!

In the Northfield Taxi Company office at Third Street and Division, Don "Fat" Lloyd was manning the two black rotary telephones, one marked 777 in the round label in the center of the dial and the other marked 444.

The company was founded in 1927 by Ray "Razzer" Otis and his two brothers with a fleet of five Cadillacs and a local telephone number of 777, chosen, no doubt, because Ray was skilled at games of chance and thought the number would bring them good luck. His fantastic memory and ability to do complicated calculations in his head no doubt were the basis for his good fortune in such games.

The company went into hibernation during WWII but was resurrected after the war when Sid Sleeth, a decorated veteran of the Pacific Campaign, bought out the old company and later upgraded its equipment by installing two-way radios that allowed cabs to get directions without returning to the office.

Fat Lloyd, after being in the taxi business for twenty years, bought out the two-car Tille Taxi

Company when brothers Theodore and Ingle decided to retire and he later bought out Sleeth's taxi business, with Sid retaining control of the charter bus operations.

Fat was relatively short, with thinning black and gray hair. He got the nickname "Fat" not for being physically overweight but because he liked to "chew the fat" or gab with nearly anyone he encountered.

Born on Valentines' Day, 1907, in Omaha, Nebraska, Don lost his father when he was a mere lad, another victim of the flu epidemic that swept the nation during World War I. His mother, Flora, and her two sons moved to Northfield to be near her sister and brother-in-law.

In high school, Fat was an extraverted young man becoming student manager of both the basketball and the football teams, as well as, acting in the Junior class play before graduating from Northfield High School. Entering the army in World War II, he served in the Seventh Division, stationed most of the time at Fort Ord in California.

Fat drank coffee continually throughout the day and night, consuming forty cups on a typical shift and smoking four packs of cigarettes each day. If someone else was acting as dispatcher while he was in the office, he would be standing against the wall, bouncing on the balls of his feet, drinking coffee, smoking a cigarette, and usually telling some funny story about "PFC Lloyd" at Fort Ord.

Fat often made some acerbic comment about one of the cab drivers, preceded by a soft throaty kind of growl – "Awrrr."

He lived with his mother and never married but frequented "classy" prostitutes in Minneapolis as needed. One of the older cab drivers attested to this fact when he said he saw him one time on the street in "The Cities" (Minneapolis and St. Paul) with an attractive woman hanging on each arm. Fat never talked about his sexual escapades but everyone in the office assumed he was conversant from his knowing laughs, grunts, and wisecracks when others told of their experiences or told stories about others.

Fat answered the ringing phone. "Taxi office," pause, "Yes ma'am. 409 East Second. Right away." Turning to Bud Odette he said, "409 East Second going to St. Olaf College."

Drivers were rotated among the different cars so that none of them could complain about getting stuck with the same junker all the time. Today Bud was driving the 1953 Plymouth, the one with the body that had dropped onto its frame so much that it was like driving a channeled hot rod, only one that lacked power and had no shocks. If you didn't slow to a crawl going over washboard roads or the railroad tracks, the chatter from the undercarriage would make your teeth rattle and your head buzz. Zack Buckler, taking a short-cut to the train depot, once drove the car, rattling and shuddering, down the Old Main Hill, a favorite sliding site for kids in the winter.

Bud pulled up at the familiar address and waited for Miss Zimmer to come out. As she descended the stairs at the front of the large two-story house, Bud reached back and unlatched the door, giving it a shove to open it all the way.

"Gutten Tage, Frauline Zimmer. Wie geht es Ihnen?" he asked in a respectful formal manner. Bud knew she was a German teacher at St. Olaf and was rumored to be a tough taskmaster in class. He liked to have an ice-breaker ready for passengers to set a positive tone for the journey and he used his limited knowledge of her discipline, garnered from his two years of college German at the University of Minnesota, with Miss Zimmer.

"Gut, danke und Ihnen?"

"Das freut mich, mir geht es auch gut," replied Bud.

Speaking into the microphone of his two-way radio, he said, "Seven going to St. Olaf." Although Fat already knew the destination, the transmission informed him of the current location of Bud on his trip in case another call came in that he could pick up on the way.

"Roger that," Fat came back on the speaker.

They rode in silence, slowing to about 10 mph as they went over the tracks, and arrived at Holland Hall about 7 minutes later, where Miss Zimmer paid her 45 cent taxi fare.

"Danke sehr," said Bud as he accepted the change and put it in his coin changer.

"Bitte, sehr," replied Miss Zimmer as she departed the cab.

"Seven is vacant at Saint O," Bud spoke into the microphone.

"Bring her back. I haven't got anything up your way," said Fat, ascribing a feminine gender to the car.

When Bud got back to the cab stand, the two parking places in front were taken and Fat uttered the command, "Put her on the side hill." So Bud went around the corner onto Third Street and a block up the hill, made a U-turn, and came back down halfway, parking at a slant in front of the Northfield Public Library, a structure made possible by a $10,000 grant to the city by Andrew Carnegie in 1908.

Entering the smoke-filled room, Bud reported his fare and it was duly recorded on the large ledger sheet by Fat. Zack Buckler had nearly fallen asleep on the couch when the next call come in. Zack was a good-looking, square-jawed crew-cut blond of average height with blue eyes, a lean and sinewy frame, and an engaging smile.

Passengers liked Zack for his kindness and sensitivity and many of them commented about it to his boss. He made special efforts to accommodate passenger needs, pick up and load their luggage, open doors, etc. He appreciated the positive regard but preferred it not be done in public or with any fanfare to make him feel conspicuous. But Zack could be moody too and fly off the handle when frustrated, after which he would return to his usual good-natured temperament, leaving on-lookers wondering what had happened.

"Awrrr. Alright, Zack. Get your ass up and go to the Corner Bar in Dundas. Johnny Olson wants to come back to town."

Zack bolted upright and flashed a hostile glare at Fat for having roused him from a pleasant dream but quickly decided not to rebel against this intrusion into his space. After all, he was getting paid to work, he thought.

"Awrrrr growled Fat. If you wouldn't chase those split-tails all night, you wouldn't have to sleep on my time."

Zack drove the three miles to Dundas and honked his horn when he pulled up to the Cor-ner Bar. Soon a tall, lanky man came stumbling down the steps. He was unshaven, wore dirty tat-tered clothes, and stunk like stale beer and sweat. Johnny climbed into the front passenger seat and requested to be taken to the bar of the same name in Northfield. Zack opened his window wide, aimed the wing window so that the wind hit his passenger, and opened the back window on his side to keep from being overpowered by the stench that was this former hero of WWI.

When they pulled up to the Northfield version of the Corner Bar at Fifth Street and Division, Zack said, "That'll be one dollar please."

Johnny fumbled in his wallet for the money and when he handed it over, let his hand drop onto

Zack's leg and left it there.

"I'm not into that shit, Johnny. Get your goddamn hand off my leg and keep it to yourself!"

Knowing that cab drivers were frequent victims of armed robberies and murder, Zack sometimes carried a 32 caliber snub-nosed revolver in a holster under his left armpit, but this was not one of those times. He had no intention of harming anyone unless absolutely necessary but wanted to make a strong enough impression on this drunken soul so that he did not attempt it again.

"Oh, so you're one of those," said Johnny.

"No, Johnny, I'm not 'One of those.' I just don't want you to be hitting on me every fucking time you call a cab. I've told you before, nicely, to pick on your friends and leave me the fuck alone. You won't like it if I get really pissed and knock you around."

"I might like that," Johnny said with a toothless grin.

"Oh for Christ's sake," said Zack, suppressing a laugh.

Getting back to the cab stand, Zack reported his fare of $1 and said, "Johnny made a pass at me, can you believe that?"

That started a round of ribbing, imagining what it would be like to get physically close to someone that smelled like the bottom of an outhouse, never bathed, and had only three teeth. The disgust reactions were so readily elicited that the conversation soon turned to something else.

Zack and Bud went outside and sat on the bench under the awning in front of the cab office. Zack had a Pall Mall and Bud rolled a Bull Durham. They had been friends since high school. Both had motorcycles. Bud bought an old 1940 Harley Davidson EL61 with a suicide clutch and virtually no brakes for $60 from the son of one of his dad's friends. Zack had a nice late model Zundapp opposed twin with shaft drive, similar to a BMW, the reputed "Best Motorcycle in the World."

They used to drag race out on the graveled back road to Dundas, next to the haunted house surrounded by trees and below the Odd Fellows Home, where Zack grew up. Bud would usually take the lead and throw the most gravel in his wake as he speed-shifted through the gears but Zack would end up the leader at the end, once he got his bike wound up to maximum RPMs. For fun, they used to "cut donuts" on the pavement by putting one foot on the ground, laying the bike at about a 45-degree angle, and dropping the clutch as the back wheel spun while the engine revved to high speeds, bolting out of the spin by plopping back on the seat and aiming in one direction. A large black circle composed of tire rubber was left to be viewed by passersby.

In high school, they used to go to the next town to the north, Farmington, hang out at the other Tiny's restaurant, try to pick up girls, and "get a little." Zack ended up going with a well-developed younger girl, Sandy, for quite a while and getting laid fairly often.

Bud rode with Judy's warm pussy pressed against his backside on the oversized motorcycle seat of his Harley but wasn't so lucky in his sexual endeavors. Every time he reached back to "cop a feel," she would take his hand and put it back on the handlebars.

Actually, he felt rather conflicted about it. Bud grew up in the poorest part of town, known as "Hungry Hollow," and was determined to escape poverty. He had been embarrassed more than once by having local merchants ask him when his father was going to pay his bill. And he detested having to ask his father for money because coming up with a rational justification for the expense was like being cross-examined by a prosecuting attorney who was convinced he was guilty. Consequently, Bud wanted to be financially independent and his route to that goal was by getting an education. And he feared being forced to abandon his quest for a college degree and the ability to make a decent living by getting some girl pregnant, having to marry her and support her and a kid. An earlier close encounter requiring Bud to sweat it out for a month before a menstrual period reappeared reminded him of the possible consequences of impulsive behavior.

Bud and Zack, convinced of the adventures possible in Colorado by a friend who had once lived there, saved a meager amount of money after graduating from high school and rode off to seek their fortune in the west. As it turned out, their "fortune" was to be working as migrant farmhands and on a threshing crew. One time, after working a ten-hour day in the hot sun, Zack urged Bud to catch up to a convertible with two beautiful girls in it to see if they could strike up a conversation. As they roared down the main street, dodging from one lane to the next to get around cars going the speed limit, they failed to see the police car trying to catch up to them. When they hit a red light, Zack stopped but Bud was going too fast to stop with his motorcycle's inadequate brakes, so he made a right turn instead. Then he saw the blinking red light behind him and decided it was no contest. To conserve their dwindling funds, Bud spent a few days in jail rather than pay the fine, while Zack found jobs for them both in a pickle factory.

Eventually, they decided there was no future in farm labor and proceeded to return home to try to get into college. But on the way, Bud's primary chain broke, ejecting through the case surrounding it, and they ended spending the night in a Nebraska ditch populated by chiggers. Thus, after a night of no sleep and bite marks all over their bodies, their adventures in the west ended.

Zack spent two years in the Army while Bud was attending St. Olaf College. When Bud transferred to the University, Zack and two other friends from high school joined them to live together in an old two-story "McKinley Horror" type house across the Minnesota River from the campus. Finally taking school seriously in order to get a decent job after graduation, they had a revolving cartoon reading "I'm so smart I make myself sick!" that hung above the desk of the one who achieved the best GPA for the quarter.

Zack dropped out when he got involved with another girl but the relationship didn't last and he returned to Northfield to get his head and heart straightened out, supporting himself by driving a cab while volunteering for the Fire Department and living above the garage where the fire trucks resided.

Bud switched his major from engineering to psychology and frequently had the cartoon hanging above his desk. Encouraged to go on to graduate school, he applied to several programs within a geographic region determined by eliminating every place with cold winters and also all of the old south, where he knew he would be killed since he could not keep his mouth shut in the face of discriminatory acts in his presence. But he was also excited about President Kennedy's newly forming Peace Corps and the adventure of living in a foreign land while contributing something to make the world a better place. So he applied to that program as well.

"Any word from the feds?" asked Zack.

"Naw. Nothing yet. I guess they have to do a background check first. I haven't heard of any FBI agents checking into my background around here yet."

"How about the graduate schools?"

"Still waiting for them too. Some of them want to have you come for an interview and I don't have enough saved to do that and still get through the first semester. I went down to see if I could take out a loan from the First National but all they wanted to know was what collateral I had. What the fuck! My dad used to get loans from Johnny Nutting all the time and he never asked for collateral, said he invested in the man, not what he had. But that was the old days. I guess they don't do things like that now."

"Fucking banks! Fucking people! They're all turning into Cash Register Minds nowadays! Whatever happened to heart? To soul? That's all gone by the wayside now. I can't make any sense out of this world anymore!"

"Yeah, it's a pisser!", agreed Bud. I'm going next door to get a cuppa. You want one?"

"Naw. I'm good."

Bud went over to the White Castle next door. He ordered a hamburger with raw onions for 25 cents and a 10 cent cup of coffee from the proprietor, Laura Baddgor. Laura had taken over the cafe from Charlie Edson, a long-time resident who helped keep the political conversations lively for all the local merchants who frequented the place. Laura, with her intelligence and brassiness, raised the level of political discourse a couple of notches higher, so it was always entertaining to hear the locals banter back and forth. She was not shy about voicing her opinions and most people respected her for her well-thought-out and bluntly stated ideas.

George Zanmiller, the mayor, was there asking what people thought about the city council's plan to close the wading pool at Way Park because of the polio epidemic, and entrenched interests voiced their opposition or support. George was amazingly calm considering the heated voices on either side of the issue and he was not provoked into committing to either side despite their emotional rhetoric.

Returning to the cab stand, Bud bit down on the hamburger, savoring the sweet onions and singed high-fat beef. "Best hamburger in town," he said to no one in particular.

Fat Lloyd was over against the wall, drinking his 20th cup of coffee and smoking his 40th cigarette while chuckling to himself about the story he just told regarding the drill sergeant at Ft. Ord who outsmarted a recruit before the novice could outsmart him. "And he says to me, 'PFC Lloyd, what do you think about that?' and I says, 'Outstanding Sergeant, outstanding!'"

Big George Triptner arrived back from meeting the Jefferson Bus at the Stuart Hotel. "Dale Halverson tried to muscle his way into the line and I had to put him down," said George.

Drivers from each company stood outside the newly arrived bus door yelling "Taxi, taxi!" to all the exiting passengers. Being first in line was always advantageous so there was a battle for being in that position. Sometimes it got physical.

The rivalry between 1100 Taxi Company and Northfield Taxi Company had been going on for years, marked by skirmishes at the train station and bus depot. Cab drivers would call in phony requests to each others' companies to divert them from where the action was. When each company got two-way radios, they would keep track of sightings of each others cabs and report them to the office. Before frequency bands became more sophisticated, they would send fake reports to each other's offices. So Dale might report "Seven is vacant in Dundas" when, in fact, Bud was at Carleton College.

Drivers from both companies referred to the police car as "Car 13" and would radio in its location to alert other drivers so they wouldn't speed if they were in that area. The message would be relayed to all drivers from the office. But drivers were not averse to tipping off police about the "reckless" driving habits of other drivers from the competing company.

"Jesus, George," exclaimed Fat. "Hope you didn't hurt him too bad when you knocked him down. Next thing you know, Pop will be calling Lenno and claiming assault or he'll come over here threatening a lawsuit!"

"Yeah, yeah," said George, feeling confident that Dale would not do anything to cause himself further embarrassment. But he could expect some sort of retaliation in the future and would have to be on guard until Dale cooled down about the incident.

There was turnover of cab drivers quite frequently when they would manage to get a higher paying job. One of the short-termers, Corn Ball, was a sometimes "jobber" who would drive around to gas stations and roadside businesses peddling "stuff." The stuff was anything that would sell, from girly mud flaps to air fresheners to various gadgets that looked like they might be a good idea. He would keep the other drivers in stitches telling stories about how he managed to cleverly convince some merchant how he could make a good return by buying a dozen copies of some half-baked invention.

Another short-termer was Tomorrow Thompson. He got his name because his parents couldn't agree on a first name for their child. When the nurse came up to them and asked the baby's name, they said they would name him tomorrow, meaning the next day. However, the nurse duly recorded the name "Tomorrow" on the record of live birth to be signed by the doctor and, once the paperwork went through it was too much trouble to change it. Tomorrow's name made for much misunderstanding and for many jokes similar to the "Who's on First" routine of Abbot and Costello. To avoid the ribbing and misunderstanding, Tomorrow called himself "Tom" but still used Tomorrow on official papers.

***

Zack went next door to Grant Electric, walked past the display of different kinds of lamps, sconces, "flying saucers" (ceiling light bulb covers) and appliances, arriving at the workspace of Lewis Norstad. Surrounded by disabled Maytag washing machines and other household devices needing repair, Lewie was at his workbench inletting a finely blued rifle barrel and Mauser action into a laminated maple and walnut gun stock that Lewie had constructed himself. Lewie was using a chisel and wood rasp and would then lay down a fiberglass blanket for the barrel and action. On the far wall, next to Willy Wolf's shoe repair work area, was a rack of exotic hunting rifles awaiting some stage of completion. On the back of the wall supporting the electric display, hung Lewie's bow and quiver with its 101st Airborne patch on it.

Looking up with a pleasing smile, Lewie said, "Hi, Zack. How's the cab business today?"

"Kinda slow, Lewie. That's a nice-looking rifle you've got going there, a .30-06?"

"Yeah. The guy that ordered it likes to shoot gophers from about 100 yards, so he wants a high-powered scope on it too. It'll make him a pretty good varmint rifle."

"I guess," said Zack. "A .30-06 will vaporize the poor little gopher that dares to poke his head up. Say, Lewie, when is the bow-hunters field competition going to be this year?" asked Zack.

"Probably in October. You and Bud going to compete this year?"

"Planing on it. Bud's the serious competitor but it's always a fun event and we get to see old friends."

Lewie had been an archery mentor to both Zack and Bud while they were in high school but the relationship with Zack covered more ground than just archery. Lewie was attuned to Zack's struggles to be manly despite his tenderhearted disposition, something Lewie knew a thing or two about after what he experienced and learned during the war.

Zack was raised in the orphanage at Odd Fellows Home after his parents were killed in an automobile accident. He looked after the younger children who lived there and would often intervene if they were picked on at school, intimidating the bullies by putting on his fierce and determined look, sometimes by punching them out.

Lewie was in a glider infantry unit attached to the 101st Airborne Division. He came ashore the second day of the invasion, fought in the Battle of the Bulge, landed in "flying coffins," engaged in hedge-row fighting in Operation Market Garden, and was involved in house-to-house fighting all the way to Berchtesgaden, Hitler's mountaintop lair in Germany.

Lewie told Zack about some of his war experiences, in bits and pieces over the years. Not an exercise in braggadocio, the incidents were presented in a matter-of-fact way, the reminiscences triggered by something they were discussing in the current day context. If Zack was talking about being frightened by something, Lewie might bring up the fear he experienced in landing behind enemy lines in a canvas-covered glider where more men were killed or injured in the landing than by the Germans. Or he might talk about a "friendly fire" incident where he was being strafed by British aircraft and fired back with his rifle.

If Zack doubted his ability to endure some particular challenge, Lewie might tell him about being pinned down for a day by a German tank or about swimming across a Dutch canal in frigid water.

If Zack felt he had made a terrible mistake, Lewie would relate the incident where he threw a hand grenade into a building during house-to-house fighting, only to discover it was occupied by an old man sitting in a rocking chair. Or he might relate the time he jumped on the back of a man crawling in the dark and was about to slit his throat when he recognized that the chin strap on his helmet was American. "Whew! Almost screwed up on that one!"

If Zack were bothered by a feeling he had to participate in some activity he disapproved of, Lewie might tell him about the time, during the Battle of the Bulge, when he disobeyed orders and captured five German infiltrators, thinking they could provide information about enemy troop dispositions. His commander retained one German officer but told Lewie to "get rid of" the other four. Feeling he had to give these men who had surrendered at least a chance at living, he took them to a clearing and told them to make a run for it and if they got to the woods before he shot them, they would be free to go. None of them made it.

The stories were not presented as lectures on morality, how to make decisions nor behavior to be emulated. They were more like, "I was confronted with this difficult situation and I survived." Or, "I had to make this decision and it turned out to be a bad one." Or, "I had to do this horrible, disgusting thing and I'll have to live with it forever. But I am still here and I learned from it." Zack appreciated the way Lewie looked at life and living and tended to idealize Lewie in spite of Lewie's denial of being any kind of hero.

"You guys coming out to the new range this weekend to help with the clearing and set-up?"

"Yeah, we'll be there. Gotta go. Fat will throw a fit if I don't get back when I'm up for a call."

3 BOWS AND ARROWS

Zack and Bud traveled down Highway 3 toward Faribault in Zack's well-preserved 1939 Plymouth businessman's coupe. Rather than making the turn into Dundas, they went up the gravel road in the opposite direction, east to a stand of trees with a little clearing just off the road where several cars were parked. Lewie's faded green 1939 Studebaker sedan was already there and its owner was talking with a group of archers ready to pitch in with the grunt-work necessary to establish and maintain a decent field archery target shooting range. A pile of hay bales had been unloaded in the clearing and there were other piles of materials necessary for the job.

The previous archery range had been abandoned because of complaints from users about the steep trails that exhausted all but the fittest and because it was situated on hills and valleys peppered with rock that broke wooden arrows and bent aluminum ones. Not only that but the frequent and unpredictable ricochets presented a hazard for other archers.

As Zack and Bud walked up to the group,

Lewie shouted out a greeting to the new arrivals. "Welcome to the clean-up and construction crew for the Cannon Valley Bow-hunters Archery Club. Good to see that you could join us on this fine summer morning. Grab a cup of coffee or soft drink over there by the table and we'll get started in a minute."

After old friends exchanged pleasantries and a few tall stories, Lewie explained the tasks that had to be accomplished.

"We've already got the locations of the fourteen targets laid out so that people can shoot and not worry that someone behind them will send an arrow into their backside. The layout is according to the standards set by the National Field Archery Association for safety. The target locations are marked on the ground with spray paint. What we have to do is place the bales of hay and secure them to the ground, pace off and locate the shooting line for targets at from 15 to 80 yards, get rid of fallen trees and branches along the pathways between targets, then rake the paths so you can walk them without tripping on anything. We'll break up into groups and each takes a different section of the course. Any questions?"

There followed a series of irrelevant and irreverent questions that got everyone into a jovial mood for the tasks ahead.

"Is there going to be entertainment at half-time?"

"Are we ready for a break yet?"

"Do we get paid minimum wage for this job?"

"Are we going to have flush toilets available for our tender bottoms?"

"Who signed me up for this gig?"

When the laughter subsided, each group set off for their particular area. Each had wheelbarrows for carting the bales of hay to their locations, rakes, pitchforks, and axes.

Some of the trees had been infected by a disease that caused them to die and their remains to be lighter than balsa wood. Zack and Bud felt like supermen as they lifted whole trees or large branches and threw them aside.

One person would cart bales of hay to the target area and then two of them would stack them so that the face of the stack was perpendicular to the shooting locations. Then they applied a waterproof sheet to the top of the stack, pounded two stakes in the ground on each end of the stack, and stretched rope tie-downs between matching stakes, cinching them down to compress the bales slightly. One of the volunteers would hold the end of a long tape measure to the front of the target while another would walk off with the other end toward the shooting line. When he reached the required distance, a stake would be pounded into the ground. Some targets had more than one shooting position for "walk-up" shooting positions.

The group took a break about noon, ate sandwiches, drank beverages prepared by wives of some of the volunteers, and participated in a lot of "lying and bragging," as Bill Douglas used to call it. Some of them decided to put up pistol targets and shoot a few arrows at one of the newly constructed backdrops. All eyes were on Bud as he would consistently slam three arrows into a tight group at 20 yards. During the winter, when they practiced in the basement gymnasium of the high school, Bud used to regularly keep his arrows in one-inch groups, frequently shooting the nocks off earlier arrows and ending up with no arrows to shoot. Other archers hesitated to lend him arrows because they knew of their likely fate.

Zack tied an old bowstring to an overhanging tree branch and attached a spent 12 gauge shotgun shell on the end about waist high. With bales of hay behind it to stop the arrows, he set the shotgun shell a-swinging and the boldest archers tried to hit it as it traversed its arc, to and fro. While most arrows went astray, Bud was able to hit it 3 out of 5 times.

"I hear some guys are thinking of sponsoring Bud for the Olympics," said one of the archers. "Think he's got a chance?"

"I don't know. It takes a lot of time and money to pull that off and wealthy backers are pretty sparse in this community. But maybe … you never know!"

When Bud heard rumors of being sponsored for the Olympics, he thought to himself, not very likely. Costs too much to train and there aren't any sponsors that well-healed in Northfield. Besides, my bow arm gives out after a lot of shooting and it's hard for me to stay on target, so I'd have to get that left arm in shape.

By mid-afternoon, everyone was exhausted, sweaty, and dirty. Zack had to rush off to take a shower, change clothes and get ready for his first date with Becky Halverson. After doing so, he called her to let her know he was on his way, then jumped on his Zundapp and headed for her parent's house on the corner of Madison and Forest Avenue.

***

Becky's parents came out to greet their daughter's suitor when he arrived and Dale, her brother, was sitting on the porch.

"Hi, Zack," said Dale. How are things over at 777?"

"Starting to pick up. How you doing at 1100?"

"OK. Pop's having some heart problems so all the guys are worried about him. How's Fat doing? Is he still drinking coffee and smoking cigarettes all day?"

"Yeah, you know Fat. He'll probably blow an artery one of these days."

The elder Halverson stepped into the porch. "How ya doing, Zack?" he said nervously as he reached out to shake his hand.

"I'm fine, sir. And you?" said Zack, trying to put Mr. Halverson at ease. "You still taking photos down at the arboretum? I saw some of your pictures in the *Northfield News* last week and they were great - very captivating."

"Yeah, they turned out pretty good but I got to get better at developing the negatives, especially the colored ones. Photography is like a tranquilizer for me – calms my nerves."

Mrs. Halverson poked her head in the doorway. "Hi Zack, You taking Becky out tonight?"

"Yeah. Thought we'd stop at Bill's Pizza and then go to a movie," said Zack.

"Oh, that should be fun," Mrs. Halverson cooed sweetly. "Just remember to get back before midnight or I'll start to worry."

"And be careful on that motorcycle," warned Mr. Halverson. "There's nothing to protect you if something goes wrong. I remember when I was a waist gunner on a B-17 and that flak could cut right through the skin of that airplane like it was butter."

"Oh, Dad," Dale said in an exasperated voice. "There's nothing to be afraid of. Zack has been riding that thing for years and hasn't had an accident."

"Don't worry, Mr. Halverson," said Zack. "We'll just be puttering along in town. I'll be careful and we'll be back before midnight."

Becky came bouncing out the door onto the porch. "OK. I'm ready. Bye, Mom. Bye Dad," as she kissed each on the cheek.

Zack parked his motorcycle in front of the Northfield National Bank on Division Street, the same place he and the other motorcyclists in their group used to park and sit perched atop their bikes, watching girls parade by after high school was out for the day. They might venture as far as the Ice Cream Shop for refreshments or to Tiny's for a pack of cigarettes before returning to their bikes.

The couple walked halfway up the block on Fourth Street to Bill's Pizza where they ordered a medium pepperoni with black olives and sat at one of the small tables.

"How's work going at your new job?" asked Zack, referring to Becky's employment at the State Bank.

"It's OK.," said Becky. "Kind of interesting. I'm mostly a teller at one of the windows handling customer requests, you know, deposits and withdrawals. You have to record all those transactions with receipts and ledger entries and resupply cash drawers when they need it. I did get to go into the vault one time today to get a customer's safe deposit box. Kinda claustrophobic in there. But it's really kind of dull work when it comes down to it."

"Can't see yourself doing that sort of thing for the next forty years?" asked Zack

"No. I'm going back to school when I can afford it, probably at St. Olaf. That's where everyone on the west side of the river goes. 'Course we're regarded as "townies" and looked down on. Carleton is for rich kids from out of town or children of faculty and staff who get a free ride. The place has a good reputation though."

"Yeah. Do you know what you want to study?"

"I'm kinda inclined toward the nursing program. I like to help people in a direct, practical way. They have connections up in Minneapolis where you can get your in-service training. And in nursing, you can always go in and out of the workforce to accommodate family needs."

"Sounds like that might be a good fit for you, Becky. I'm still floundering around, trying to find a place where I fit. I don't know what I'm good at. I did OK. in school but nothing grabbed me. I did OK. in the army too but don't much care for killing people. But it was fun as hell in training to blow stuff up. That was a real blast!"

Becky laughed. "I suppose you could be a demolitions man. 'Course you'd have to move around for that – probably not enough business in a place like Northfield to keep you employed all the time."

"They could call me 'Boom-boom Buckler'," said Zack. "Call Boom-boom to make all your troubles disappear!" he laughed. "Naw, I want a job with a purpose, something more than a paycheck, something that contributes to a cause greater than myself. Life is too short to spend it collecting money and stuff. I liked helping the kids at Odd Fellows grow up and become whatever they wanted to be. I know people are complicated but it is fascinating to help them discover what they have to offer. What I don't want is to work some hum-drum nine-to-five job under the supervision of a rigid, dictator-like boss."

When they finished their pizza, Becky and Zack

walked the half-block up the hill to the Grand Theater where *South Pacific* was playing. Sliding a dollar bill through the window, Zack obtained two tickets before they entered the lobby. A well-dressed man with finely trimmed gray hair and mustache, looking every bit the impresario, approached and offered up his hand to Zack.

"Hello, Zack. Good to see you again."

"Hi, Mr. Olson. Dinger, this is my friend Becky Halverson."

"Oh, how nice to meet you, Miss Halverson. I hope the two of you enjoy the movie. They finally got the rental price down far enough so we could bring it to town. It has been a smash hit in the big cities," said Dinger.

After a stop at the refreshment counter for popcorn and boxes of Milk Duds and Juju Beans, they entered the darkened theater and found seats in one of the elevated boxes along the sides of the old Ware Auditorium, which dated back to 1899.

"I didn't know that you knew Mr. Olson on a first name basis," said Becky.

"Yeah, he comes into the cab office every now and then and talks with Fat and the guys. Friendly guy. I remember when he used to give out prizes to us kids when we rode our bikes down to the free Saturday morning westerns over at the West Theater. That was before they tore it down to make way for Highway 3. Loved those old movies with Roy Rodgers, Gene Autry, Lash La Rue, Tom Mix, Hoppy, The Cisco Kid and Poncho, Gabby Hayes,

Sky King. The weekly serials they ran with them always left you on the edge of your seat."

The lights dimmed and the movie began with color filters enhancing the emotions displayed on the screen. Mitzi Gaynor as Nellie Frobush belted out *"I'm Gonna Wash That Man Right Out of My Hair"* while Rossano Brazzi as Emile mouthed the words to *"Some Enchanted Evening"* and Ray Walston made everyone laugh with *"There Is Nothing Like A Dame."* Becky reached for Zack's hand for a squeeze during love scenes and both got misty-eyed when hearts were broken.

As the couple left the theater, skipping down the sidewalk on Fourth Street, they sang excerpts from songs that left the greatest impression.

"That was a marvelous movie," said Becky. "I wish I could see it again!"

"I liked it too. Brought out some of the subtleties of racial prejudice. Nice music, of course."

Mounting Zack's motorcycle, they headed toward Becky's house on Forest Avenue but made a detour to the swings at Longfellow Elementary School.

"I went to grade school here. Had a big fight over there," said Zack as he pointed toward the northeast corner. "Can't remember what it was about but there must have been ten guys involved. I punched one of them in the nose and he got a nosebleed. Caught hell from my dad for that. That was before he and my mom were killed in an auto accident."

"I didn't know that about you," said Becky. "Is that when you were placed in Odd Fellows?"

"Yeah. My aunts and uncles couldn't take me and were fighting about the estate, so the court placed me there. It was supposed to be temporary but ended up being until I graduated from high school and got a job. I cried a lot for the first year but then got used to it. There were other kids there and it was my job to look out after them – make sure they bathed, got down to dinner, went to school, kept up with their studies – stuff like that. It tied me down a little but it gave me a purpose and made me stay focused. Probably kept me out of trouble. The older people that lived there were always available to give advice and suggestions. They had a lot of interesting and funny stories to tell. Some were pretty snotty but everyone knew who they were and avoided them."

"My dad has had a lot of nervous trouble since he came back from the war," said Becky. "He flew in bombing raids over Germany. A lot of them got shot down and sometimes they dropped their bombs on the wrong targets. That still bothers him. My mom tries to keep everything calm and predictable at home so he doesn't get rattled. But my brother, Dale, is embarrassed by it and keeps doing stupid things to show him there is nothing to be afraid of, but it just makes matters worse."

"There are a lot of guys in town that were in the war. Some of them, like your dad, saw things, did things, that continue to haunt them. Some were broken by it and turned into drunken old sots. Some, like my boss, never saw any combat and found it easy to just resume their normal lives. And some, like Lewie, seem to have learned valuable lessons about themselves and the world that make them better people for having gone through it. But I know I never want to go to war, even if it can build character, as they say. I don't like to hurt people unless it is absolutely necessary. I don't think there is any glory to war and I think it is a complete waste of human life and our natural resources. It's just plain stupid!"

"Yes, I agree but what do you do when some crackpot, like Hitler, decides to invade and take over your country or does cruel and brutal things, inhumane things? People like that don't listen to reason and you can't just let them get away with their atrocities."

"You're right about that, Becky, and I guess if that happened again, I'd have to do my part to stop them but I wouldn't take any pleasure in killing and maiming the poor slobs who got duped into following their leader. What we need is for all the countries in the world to choose knowledgeable leaders who can seek reasonable solutions and negotiate with each other to arrive at compromises. And for that to happen, we need well-educated citizens who can evaluate the strengths and weaknesses of those who are vying to be leaders and make good estimates of how they would handle the issues facing them. Now that I say it, it sounds kind of idealistic doesn't it?"

"Yes," said Becky as she leaned over and kissed Zack on the cheek, "but I like your idealism and wouldn't want you to give it up. Just don't expect all the required things for it to take place to happen any time soon."

Zack gazed into Becky's soulful eyes, seeing a sympathetic but practically-minded counterpart. After all the girls he had been with, was this the one that might be a good fit for him, he wondered. No, it's too soon, too soon, he thought. Go slow and don't screw it up this time.

Finally, Zack said, "We better get you home or your dad will be waiting for me with a shotgun in hand."

4 THE LAY OF
THE LAND

Milt and his gang assembled at a spot on Union Lake, seven miles west of town, where their assemblage was not likely to be seen as anything out of the ordinary. Milt brought a case of beer and all brought fishing gear to mislead any onlookers as to their intentions. Everyone had a beer in hand and some munched on Frito's.

"Alright, listen up guys," said Milt as he interrupted the ongoing chit-chat. "I thought we'd meet out here so we can talk about something important without worrying about being overheard. As you know, we've been pretty successful with our little raids on the college student population. We've pulled off nine of them without a hitch, so far. And we've made a little spending money and had a lot of fun doing it."

"Yea, Milt!" shouted out Clarence. The others grunted their support but picked up their ears when Milt announced:

"Now is the time for us to graduate into something more lucrative but also more risky. I've been eying the State Bank for over a year and I think we should rob it."

Jaws went agape, eyes popped in the members of the assembled crew. Everyone started to say, "Wha..." at the same time.

"Holy shit! We'll all end up serving hard time at Stillwater," said an agitated Billy.

"Calm down and listen to Milt," said Clarence. "He's brought us through all our earlier capers and we haven't got caught yet. He deserves our respect."

"Do you really think we are good enough to pull it off?" asked Dale. "I mean we are a bunch of hicks from the sticks. None of us are any Carl Gugasian or Bonnie and Clyde, or even Jesse James, for Chris's sake."

"You guys remember Willie Sutton?" asked Milt rhetorically.

"Yeah, I remember that article about him in the *Minneapolis Star* a few years ago," said Dale. "It was headlined 'Willie has friends' and reported the murder of the young guy who ratted him out and then bragged about it on TV."

"Yeah, That's the guy," said Milt. "But he never killed anybody and he only used guns as props, they were never loaded. It was the Gambino Family that rubbed out the rat. Willie only went through eighth grade but his bank-robbing career lasted 40 years and he got away with about $2 million! He spent a lot of time in jail and the police beat the shit out of him once trying to get him to confess, but he never did. And he escaped three times! When he got too old for that, he helped other prisoners with their legal cases.

"He was one smart and crafty sonofabitch! He wore disguises and one time robbed a bank dressed as a police officer. He was even dressed down by a superior officer on the way to the bank because he had a button unbuttoned! Can you believe that? Talked his way out of it. He wrote a book about his life and even composed a song!

"So don't give me any shit about being from Bumfuck, Minnesota and not knowing anything. You can learn just like Willie did."

"Didn't he say that he robbed banks because that was where the money was?" asked Billy.

"He denied ever saying that," said Milt. "What he did say was that he loved doing it. It made him feel more alive than at any other time in his life. He enjoyed everything about it so much that he was antsy to get on with the next job."

"John Dillinger was my hero," said Clarence. "He robbed 24 banks and even stuck up four police stations! The newspapers loved his colorful personality and painted him as a kind of Robin Hood. But Hoover hated him and used his exploits to get the FBI going."

"And then there was Pretty Boy Floyd and Baby Face Nelson," said Howard. "Woody Guthrie wrote a song about Floyd and one of the characters in the Dick Tracy comic strip was based on him."

"I read that Nelson's real name was Lester Gillis

and he was a short man with a handsome face," said Dale. He killed more FBI agents than anyone else ever did. His gang and the Dillenger Gang were at a lodge in Wisconsin when the FBI got tipped off and began a raid. Nelson attacked them head-on, shooting at Melvin Purvis before the other agents could get organized. Then he made it out the back of the lodge, kidnapped a couple and got them to drive him to another house, and then stole another car. The FBI stopped him but he shot his way out of it and stole the FBI car! And Dillenger got away too. Bad day for the FBI."

"Alright, enough with the celebrity talk. Let's hear the plan," said Howard. "We can't decide whether or not we can do it if we don't know the details."

"Howard's right," said Milt. "And we are here to start working out a plan and filling in the details. But I think we can do it if we put our heads together, determine what it will take to do it, and see if we have the skills and resources to pull it off."

"OK. First, we need to decide whether to go in at night when no one is there or to do a daylight job," said Howard. "If we were to go in at night, we'd have to figure out how to disable the alarm system, if there is one. Then we'd have to figure out if we go through the only door to the building, or through the windows over the river, or through the dome on top."

"And once we got in, we'd have to figure out how to open the vault and safe," said Milt.

"I wonder how that dome is attached to the top of the building, said Howard. "It's probably heavy as hell and all of us together wouldn't be able to move it, once it was detached. Maybe we could cut a section of it away so we could descend by ropes but I'd be afraid of the whole damn thing falling in on top of us."

"Sounds too risky," said Dale,

"I sure as hell wouldn't drop through a fractured skylight," said Billy.

"So, the dome option doesn't seem possible, said Milt. "How about the windows over the river?"

"Here again, we'd have to drop down from the roof on ropes, break the windows into the basement, and hope there is a way back up to the vault that we can get through," said Howard. "The other option would be to come up from the river by an extension ladder. If the water is low enough, we could anchor the ladder on the riverbed. But if the water flow is fast and high enough, it would push the ladder over and we'd end up in the drink!"

"We could use one of those things they used in the war to fire a hook with a rope attached to it up to the roof," said Clarence.

"No way," said Dale. "Even if we were able to get one of those things from military surplus, people would hear us firing it off and we'd end up halfway up the wall with spotlights on us."

"Looks to me like the only feasible way is through the front door," said Milt. "Now, at night, it would be locked and there probably is an alarm, so we'd have to be able to unlock the door and disable the alarm. So Billy, write this down: we need to find out the location of the wires leading to the alarm. As for getting through the door, does anyone know what kind of lock they have on it?"

No one spoke, so Milt said "Someone needs to go over there and take a look at the door lock without looking suspicious. Write that down, Billy."

"We could blow it but that would make a lot of noise," said Clarence. "But we've got an acetylene torch over at the garage that can cut through almost anything and is pretty quiet."

Milt said, "Billy, put acetylene torch under the heading of 'Resources'. We may need to acquire more resources before we are through. I'm also thinking we need to get more information on several things before we can proceed with the planning of this caper."

Everyone was onto their second or third beer by now and the enthusiasm for the project was growing, tempered by Billy's anxiety and Dale's skepticism.

"I agree," said Howard. "Let's make a list of what we need to know in order to plan how to make it work. First, we need to know where the alarm is and how to disable it. Second, we need to know about the lock on the front door and how to get through it. Third, we need to know how to get into the vault and the safe. Oh, I just thought, we need to know how much money is in the tellers' drawers in case we can't get into the vault. And what about the safe-deposit boxes? Can we gain access to those once we are in the vault?"

"And just in case we decide to make a daylight entry, we need to know who will be there, at what time, and the schedule for the armored car deliveries and pick-ups," said Milt.

"Do we know anyone that works there?" said Howard.

"My sister just started working there," said Dale. "But I don't want her to get involved in this. She's a straight arrow and she'd probably turn us in if she knew what we are planning. I might be able to eavesdrop on what she tells my parents about her work and I may be able to ask some innocent questions to get at information we need."

"Good, you do that Dale," said Milt. "I'll go over there and open a bank account and scout out the place inside. Clarence, you keep a record of who comes and goes in that door, since you have a good view of it, and note when the armored car arrives, how long it stays, and when it leaves. I'll try to do that too from my vantage point at the bar and then we can compare our records and take averages. Howard, you have the most technical skill so see if you can find out about that front door. I'll get the names and numbers off the vault and give them to you so you can look up the specifics on them. Billy, if any of those bankers come into your place for lunch or snacks, see if you can learn about any upcoming events. But be cool about it, for god's sake."

By this time, everyone was getting a buzz on

and the conversation dissolved into a lot of lying and bragging. The "fishermen" decided to forgo the pleasures of fishing and instead polished off the case of beer.

*****

The next day, Milt went over to the State Bank and opened a savings account, depositing $20. Entering the circular lobby, he noted the colored glass ceiling of the dome and the terrazzo floor. Eight pillars held up wooden beams and a chandelier hung from the ceiling over a tall circular customer signing table. All the woodwork had a dark mahogany finish. On the right were three brass tellers windows and an office for the cashier. On the street side were a board room and private consultation room. There was a seat carved into the wall as well as an alcove where customers could examine their safe deposit boxes or conduct other requirements of their banking tasks with some degree of privacy.

The vault was situated across from the board room. Milt wanted to get a better look.

"Do you suppose I could rent a safe deposit box as long as I am here? I don't have anything to put in it right now but I have some important papers at home that I'd like to keep safe," he asked the cashier who was handling his savings account.

"Certainly, Mr. Grubbs. What size would you like?"

"I don't know. What sizes do you have? Could I

take a look at them?"

"Sure. Come on over to the vault. It's tight but I think we can both fit in here. These here are the sizes we have. The smallest is three by five inches and the largest is 10 by 15 inches. The bigger the box the higher the price."

"I think the four by ten is big enough for me," said Milt.

"You should know that the contents of safe deposit boxes are not insured," said the clerk. "So we discourage people from putting cash or other liquid assets in them but some people do so anyway. It is not illegal. The boxes are just as safe as anything else in the vault except for the safe. "

"I see," said Milt. "And what is this vault made of anyway?"

"It has steel girders an inch apart in the floor and ceiling and then filled with concrete. The side walls are a foot and a half of concrete plus a layer of brick and it extends down into the basement. The steel door weighs two tons."

"Amazing," said Milt. "Only an idiot would try to get in there. What about the safe?"

"That's even more impenetrable," said the clerk. It weighs 5000 pounds and has a double time-lock."

"Time lock? Isn't that what Heywood told the James Gang that the First National had so he couldn't open the safe?"

"That's it," said the teller. "Only this one is a double. They had only a single. And it wasn't even set when the gang tried to get in. Heywood was running a big bluff and they went for it!" she laughed.

As they left the vault, Milt tried to memorize the name of the manufacturer: "Hastenbach-Morrsch! Hastenbach-Morrsch!," he said to himself over and over.

***

Milt kept watching the goings-on at the bank across the street, jotting down notes on a tablet below the counter using a code of his own making so that, if it were discovered, the reader wouldn't be able to make any sense of it. Clarence did likewise from his position at the Flying A, taking his notes on a spiral notebook he kept in his overalls. After a few weeks of keeping notes, they got together to compare results.

"The tellers and the cashier usually arrive at 8:00 am and go home at 5:00 pm, sometimes later," said Milt. "The president moseys in sometime in the later morning. The front door gets locked at 3:00 pm. The board of directors shows up once a month on the last Friday or for some special meeting that is called."

"That armored car seems to come on any workday of the week and anytime between 9:00 am and 3:00 pm," said Clarence.

"Doesn't make any sense to me. They must just call when they need it, not on any fixed schedule," said Milt.

"Customers can arrive at any of those times but the times that are busiest are around 11:00 in the morning and 2:00 in the afternoon," said Clarence.

"Those are probably businesses making deposits from the previous day or at the end of the current day before the bank closes," said Milt. "The trickle of customers other times are probably those coming in to try to get loans or make payments of one sort or another. So we can't tell from this when the bank is loaded with dough or when it is empty. We may have to rely on Dale to get that information from his sister. But, if we were to pull a daylight job, it would be best to do so before 11:00 or maybe just before they close."

***

Milt was particularly watchful of any employees, hoping they might come over for a beer so he could weasel information out of them. That didn't happen because they were instructed to be mindful of the banks and their positions in the community. Sober, serious, and dependable was the impression they were to create for the investing class of the community.

Milt felt fate had taken a lucky twist one day when a drunken late-night patron sat down at his bar. Teddy Pitt had worked for Hermann Schmidt in his septic tank pumping business and thought he deserved a raise but Hermann, being a tight-fisted old German, thought he could replace Teddy with a poor farm kid who had dropped out of school and increase his profit thereby.

"That fuckin' old kraut!" said Teddy. "I slaved for that sonofabitch for five years and that's the credit I get! Smelling that crap all day and getting it all over your clothes. It's not like he can't afford it. He's got more money than J. Paul Getty."

"You don't say," said Milt. "Pumping shit is as lucrative as pumping oil?"

"That's a good one," slurred Teddy with a laugh. "Naw. I don't know where he got it but he told me once that he had over $100,000 in that bank over there," as he pointed at the window toward the State Bank.

"You don't say," said Milt as a smile graced his face. "You mean he has a savings account with $100,000 in it?"

Teddy burped and swung his hand in a half-circle above his head. "Naw. That's not it. He's got it in bearer bonds in a safe deposit box."

"What the hell are bearer bonds," asked Milt.

"I don't know for sure. They're supposed to be like ordinary bonds that pay interest and can be bought and sold. The thing about them is that bearer bonds don't have any registered owner – they are 'a-nony-mouse' so they are just like cash. If you lose them or they burn up in a fire, you're just shit out of luck."

"You don't say," said Milt yet again. "Well isn't that interesting. Been nice talking with you, Teddy. Do you want me to call you a cab to go home? Hey, better yet, why don't I introduce you to a nice girl that can push all your troubles into the background, give you a fresh perspective on life." Catching Des's eye, he summoned her over to meet Teddy.

"Des, this here is Teddy and he could use some of your ministrations to ease his troubled mind. He's had a bad day and will be a grateful friend to us both."

"I always aim to please," said Des as she put Teddy's arm around her shoulder and led him out the door.

Milt debated with himself about revealing the information he had obtained to the rest of the gang, finally deciding to forgo any such disclosure until he determined if it was really necessary.

5 THE TRENCH-COAT MAN

Fat was up against the back wall, drinking a cup of coffee and smoking a cigarette when Mayor Zanmiller walked in.

"Hi, George. What's the city up to today?" said Fat.

"That's what I came in here to find out," chuckled the mayor. "You guys see what's really going on in the community. I just run into blowhard businessmen who are trying to convince me of some position that will benefit them."

"Yeah, we can tell you whose business is doing good, whose is having hard times, who's getting drunk, who's stepping out on their spouse, who has a gripe going against who, whose kids are getting into trouble, whose are winning awards," said Fat. "We're the gossip pipeline of Northfield."

George looked directly at Fat and said, "Come on outside with me for a minute. I've got something to ask you." Zack and Bud looked at each other with a questioning "What's up?' expression.

Outside on the bench where both were sitting,

George said, "Fat, we've got a problem in town and it's not pool. Chief Brandt tells me some college kids have reported being robbed by a gang of bandits. It's happened when they have been walking back to campus from downtown. Both St. Olaf and Carleton. A gang of four or five step out of the bushes and hold a gun and a baseball bat on them and demand all their money. Luckily, no one has been hurt so far but that could happen."

"How many robberies have there been?" asked Fat.

"We've had seven reports, so far and the word is that there have been more who haven't reported it. Of course, the school administrators are putting pressure on us to find and arrest the perpetrators but they don't want a lot of publicity – worried it might affect enrollment for next year."

"Reminds me of the 'hypo-Harry' incidents a few years ago when this guy was running around Norway Valley scaring the shit out of St. Olaf girls. Some of the victims claimed he was chasing them with a hypodermic syringe."

"Yeah, they never did find him. Just disappeared and wasn't heard from again – probably some college prankster. But these crimes involve several individuals brandishing weapons. They could be dangerous and we, the city, need your help in trying to find out who they are."

"Of course," said Fat. "What do you want us to do?"

"Well, if you could have a couple of your trusted

drivers keep their eyes peeled for anything strange or unusual going on, keep an eye on students walking the streets toward their colleges, eavesdrop on their passengers' conversations for any clues, ask some of the down and outers they know if they have heard any scuttlebutt about the robberies. Then, if they pick up anything, you can relay it to me. But tell them to be discreet so we don't get a bunch of rumors going around town and citizens clamoring for action."

The mayor walked across the street to the old YMCA building, currently City Hall and home of the Northfield Police Department. Fat went inside the cab stand where Zack and Bud were the only drivers present.

"Boys, the mayor wants us to help him and the police catch some assholes that are robbing college students walking between town and their campuses."

Fat proceeded to give them the story about the robberies and their role as information gatherers. Both were excited to be playing detective and eagerly agreed to pay special attention to activities on the streets and pick up any clues they could from passengers. They also volunteered to blend into the crowds at various haunts during their off-hours and see what they could pick up.

***

Clarence, on a break from his job at Flying A, walked over to the center of the Fourth Street

Bridge to have a cigarette. Squint Howard, a dis-abled WWI veteran, and career alcoholic was there, also having a cigarette and watching the cars going by.

"How's it going Squint, ol' buddy," said Clarence, presuming Squint would be honored by someone other than one of the town characters talking to him.

"Whaddafuck, whaddafuck," mumbled Squint. "Tough times a-coming! Tough times a-coming! Just you wait, you'll see!"

"What the hell are you talking about, you old coot? Things are going fine for me. I just got me a new car, well, a new second-hand car. And I got me a raise. And I got me a pal, Milt. He's one hell of a guy and he thinks I am pretty special too. Why we're going to make this town wake up and salute one of these days. Yes, sir, that's what we're going to do. You can count on it."

Squint cast a sideways glance at Clarence, think-ing he was a total pompous ass. Then he pushed himself off the guard rail he was leaning against, uttered something unintelligible, and walked away.

**

Bud got a call to pick up Squint Howard at the local Corner Bar. He had known Squint for years and respected him for his service in The War to End All Wars. He knew that Squint got his nick-name from a farming accident involving a pitchfork. He also knew that, more recently, Squint had gotten into a pitchfork fight with another friend, Fred Ferguson, while working together and wondered if it was the same kind of fight that cost him his eye. Unlikely, he thought, since he and Fred became good friends afterward.

"Hi, Mr. Howard. Where to?"

"Dundas, Corner Bar," came the reply.

Once they got on the highway, Bud asked if Squint might be willing to keep his ears and one good eye attuned to any unusual goings-on in the circles in which he traveled and let him know what was going down.

"Is this about those college student robberies?"

"You've heard about them?" asked a surprised Bud.

"Yeah, I've heard. Don't know who's doing it though. Heard some whispers here and there."

"Will you do it? And let me know if you learn anything?"

"Sure, but you gotta make this a free ride to Dundas."

Bud laughed. "Well, OK. But keep mum about what you hear and be careful what you say. These guys may be dangerous."

"Danger, spanger, Lone Ranger! I've had more lead thrown at me than anyone in this town will ever know! Couldn't be any worse than that. But I'll keep my mouth shut and signal you from my office on the bridge when you drive by."

"Thanks, Squint. I appreciate it. I know you survived the big one," said Bud. "Be careful."

**

"Zack, I've got a call for you to handle, said Fat. "Go to the train depot and pick up a guy named Claude Thornton who wants a ride to Dundas."

Zack parked in the lot on the north side of the railroad station and went inside, where he saw the telegrapher and a man wearing a trench coat and a camel-colored tear-drop fedora seated on a bench in the waiting area.

"Mr. Thornton?" said Zack.

"Yes," said the man.

"You called for a cab?"

"Oh, yes I did. You're the driver?"

"That's me," said Zack. "Do you just have that one suitcase?"

"Just the one. I'll hold onto my briefcase."

Zack picked up the suitcase and lead the man out to the taxi, placing the suitcase in the trunk. "You want to sit in front or in the back?" asked Zack.

"I'll sit in front, thank you. Always want to see where I'm going."

"Where in Dundas do you want to go?" asked Zack.

"Oh, just take me to the center of town and I'll figure it out from there."

Once on the road, Zack inquired of the taciturn stranger, "Here on a visit or for business?"

"A little of both, I guess."

"What kind of business are you in?" asked Zack, always interested in learning about different occupations and their characteristics in his effort to find one for himself.

"I do investigations."

"Criminal type investigations?" asked Zack.

"I used to do that. Now I'm more into the private variety."

"That must be an interesting kind of work," said Zack, hoping the guy would elaborate.

"Yeah, sometimes. You never know how it will turn out. Sometimes it can get pretty dicey, sometimes people get mad at you and give you a bad time."

"You looking into any problems down here?"

"I can't talk about that. Are there any difficulties down here that I should know about?"

"Well, maybe. Someone has been causing problems with some of the college students."

"Maybe I'll check that out." Arriving at their destination, he gave Zack the fare plus a tip and said, "What's your name again?"

" Zack, Zack Buckler."

***

On Friday night when he was off duty, Zack drove down to 3D – Dundas Dine and Dance, a honky-tonk with loud music, lots of dancers, abundant alcoholic beverages, and little dining. It was a rowdy place with fist-fights not uncommon. They usually didn't last long inside as two burly bouncers would swiftly descend upon them and throw the rule violators out the door.

Zack drove into the gravel parking lot and parked his car as far away from other vehicles as possible, assuming some drunken driver would be bound to smash into something as he departed. The noise was deafening as he showed the gate-keeper his ID and entered the door.

"Gimme a Bubs," he said to the bartender, ordering a brew bottled in Faribault. He took his beer and sauntered over to the side wall, off the dance floor, where he spotted Dale Halverson, Becky's brother.

"Haven't seen you here before," said Dale. "What's the occasion?"

"This is my first time here. Just thought I would check it out. Sure is loud. I can't hear myself think!"

"Yeah, that's 3D for you! Hey, look over there – a guy just bumped into some guy's girlfriend and made her spill her drink. Now the boyfriend has to show off in front of his girl - going to start a fight, I'll bet you a dollar!"

Sure enough, even though the bumper apologized to the girl and offered to buy her another drink, the boyfriend had to demonstrate his manhood to the gathering audience that was cheering him on. The bumper backed away a little and said he didn't want to fight but the boyfriend would have none of it and took a wild swing, throwing himself off balance when his fist met nothing but the smoke-filled air.

"I think it would be best if you just went over and sat down with your girl," said the bumper.

"Why you scrawny sonofabitch. I'll knock your head off," said the boyfriend as he took another swing. First thing you know, the boyfriend was on the floor, gasping for air and the bumper had his right arm twisted into a pretzel.

"Now are you going to be a good little boy and give up this fight or do I have to put your arm in a sling for the next month?" said the bumper.

"I give, I give," said the boyfriend as he grabbed his shoulder in pain. His girlfriend came up to him and begged him to leave, which he did without any resistance. The bouncers arrived but the altercation was over as fast as it began.

"Who was that masked man?" asked Dale alluding to a phrase made famous in a popular TV western.

Zack recognized the bumper as Donny Clark, a graduate of Northfield High School a couple of years before him. He was undefeated in competitions as a wrestler and was known for discombobulating his opponents by drinking beer or smoking cigarettes before a match such that he was quite aromatic when on the mat. Currently, he was said to be a member of a group calling themselves "Fubar," the WWII military acronym for "Fucked Up Beyond All Repair." Zack had heard of the group but didn't know the members personally.

Recently, Clark and two other members of the

group had been in a kerfuffle over at Mike & Al's Bar and outside at John & Lil's Cafe. Two of them were threatened with a police blackjack and arrested. The third, Lars Kindem, known as Argo, had been shot at by the untrained constable even though he was not involved in the altercation. In the ensuing trial, it came out that Clark's great offense was that he swore in the bar when the owner refused to serve him and snapped the suspenders of the proprietor of the cafe when he threatened him with a citizen's arrest. All Fubar members were found not guilty in the subsequent official trial.

But they were involved in a brawl, the law was called and this guy seems pretty scrappy, Zack thought. Maybe they could be behind the robberies.

Zack danced with a couple of girls and talked with several people he knew but heard nothing suggesting anyone knew any robberies were taking place. Since he was already in Dundas, he decided to check out the rest of the town, meaning the two other bars and the cafe. No clues drifted his way through the clamor of the bars but he did note the trench coat man talking to the proprietor of the cafe when he stopped in for a cheeseburger. They made eye contact but didn't speak.

***

The next week a drunken passenger asked Bud if he had heard anything about a Carleton student being robbed on the way to her dormitory.

"No, I didn't hear about that," said Bud. "How did you hear about it?"

"One of the bartenders at Mike & Al's was talking with someone about it. Don't know who it was – never saw him around here before."

Zack got a call from one of the two St. Olaf College girls running the Viking Cafe on First and Madison Streets. Both of them were flirtatious with Zack every time they saw him.

"When are you going to give me a ride on your motorcycle, Zack?" Jennifer murmured.

Zack was ambivalent about getting romantically involved with either or both girls. On the one hand, they were attractive, sexy, and brash, which stirred his passions. A quick romp in the hay without any strings attached was certainly not an opportunity to miss out on. But there were always strings, even if the girls said there were none, they were just hidden. Zack's passions had led him astray in previous encounters, culminating in disaster for ongoing relationships. If he was going to go with Becky, he should at least stay true to her until he knew whether or not it would work out, even though they had not committed to going steady.

"We'll see. Maybe one of these days," said Zack, not closing the door to future possibilities. "Where do you want to go?"

"Down to Jacobsons. I need to get some stuff for the cafe. Anything important going on in town?"

"Well, kinda. You hear anything about St. Olaf students having trouble walking home from town?"

"You mean the robberies? Yeah, some Oles were talking about it the other day in the cafe. At least no one has been hurt. Some of the girls are really scared. Funny that there hasn't been anything in the paper about it, not even in the *Manitou Messenger*."

"I think they're trying to keep it quiet so they don't scare off any new applicants. It's both St. Olaf and Carleton students, so it could be a big hit economically for the schools as well as the city. A couple of us cab drivers have been asked to see if we can ferret out any clues as to who might be doing it. Do you have any idea who might be behind it?"

"Not really. My partner, Sue, thought it might be a prank pulled by some of our students but I doubt that. What student would want to risk his whole future for an unlawful prank? College student buffoonery this isn't! This is too serious."

***

The next time Zack saw the trench-coat man was when he hauled him from Dundas back to the railroad depot from which he originated. He was just as laconic as before but, as he was paying his fare, he said to his driver, "Zack, I bet the people that you are looking for are members of the Fubar gang. Mark my words, that's an opinion based on years of experience."

"How do you know that," asked Zack.

"I've got my sources. I can't divulge them but they can be trusted. See you next time I'm in town," said the mysterious stranger as he donned his fedora and disappeared into the depot to await the next train out of town.

When Zack got back to the office he asked Fat if he knew a guy who wore a trench coat and fedora and spent time in Dundas.

"Yeah, I know him. He comes down here from The Cities by train about once a year and spends a few days in Dundas before going back home. I think his mother lives in Dundas."

"Is he really a detective? Did he work for the FBI? He acts like a spook and doesn't talk very much. "

"Oh, I don't know about that," said Fat chuckling. Is that what he told you?"

"Yeah, and he claims that he has it on good authority that it is a gang that calls themselves 'Fubar' that is behind these robberies. Do you know anything about them? I know that Donny Clark is one of them and about a week ago I saw him take down a guy at 3D in a flash. I mean, this guy might actually be violent. "

"No, I don't know them but you know who you might check with is Fat Freddie Ferguson. He knows a lot of those west-side guys."

6 THINKING LIKE A FISH

Zack didn't know Fat Freddie Ferguson personally but Bud had mentioned him in earlier conversations. The two of them had known each other since they were young teens, often going hunting and fishing together. Freddie was an outstanding fisherman, even at a young age. Bud recounted stories where Freddie would reel in sunfish after sunfish down on one of the islands at Carleton Lake while Bud was skunked.

"You have to think like a fish," Fat Freddie would always say. "Then you can figure out how to catch them."

Bud could never become a "fish-head" even though his father had the same talent as Fat Freddie.

"Fat Freddie" earned his name by being nearly 300 pounds while still in high school. His four siblings also made a substantial presence. Their mother, a former nurse, worried about the adverse effects of their excess weight but that did not stop her from creating the most sumptuous meals and delightful Christmas cookies. His father, a very kind, soft-spoken but somber man, came to Northfield with nothing but a twelve-gauge shotgun yet managed to build a successful business even though he secretly suffered from chronic depression.

Freddie was a friendly bloke and always liked to hang out with older guys. He was eager to please and first to offer assistance if it was needed. Zack found him at his father's place of business, cleaning and straightening up.

"Hi, you Freddie?" asked Zack.

"Ya, fer sure I am Fred Ferguson," said Freddie, exaggerating a Swedish accent.

"I'm Zack Buckler. Fat Lloyd suggested I talk with you."

"Fat Lloyd, huh! That guy is a different breed of fat."

Zack smiled at the self-mocking joke. "He said you were likely to know something about the Fubar Gang."

"Gang?" asked Fat Freddie in disbelief. "I don't think I'd call them a gang – more like an association of like-minded, boisterous, and cocky creatures who sometimes do things just to shock the stodgy old farts in town."

"Would you consider them to be dangerous?" asked Zack.

Another incredulous look from Fat Freddie. "Dangerous? Are you kidding me? They're all St. Olaf students, a lot of them good old Northfield boys. One of them is in the choir. They dig the same songs, poetry, literature, and music. They're eccentrics, mavericks, truth and beauty seekers. They're kinda like the beatniks. They reject the usual social rules and are into creative expression. They're about as likely to hurt someone as is Albert Schweitzer or the Dali Lama."

"How about Donny Clark? I saw him take down a bigger guy at 3D a while back. He put the hurt on him as fast as greased lightning. He looked like he could hurt somebody real bad."

"Oh, Donny. Yeah, he could hurt somebody if he really wanted to. But I have never heard of him getting into a fight with some asshole who didn't deserve it. Did you know that his dad's a professor at St. Olaf?"

"No. Didn't know that," said Zack. "So you believe that it would be pretty unlikely that these Fubar guys would pull off armed robberies?"

"Armed robberies? Whoa! When was that?" asked Fat Freddie."

"Yeah, some guys, maybe four or five, have been sticking up college students between downtown and their campuses. Had guns and clubs. People are worried. Let me know if you hear anything will ya?"

"Ya for sure," said Fat Freddie. "Give Bud my regards when you see him."

Bud had been off a few days and Zack had not had a chance to share his suspicions about the Fubar Gang. He mentioned his conversation with Fat Freddie.

"I think he's right," said Bud. "They aren't the

kind of guys who'd be pulling armed robberies. I gave the trench coat guy a ride to Dundas last year. I call him 'Sam Spade,' the make-believe detective. I think he's just a bull-shitter trying to make himself look important. More than likely, he's been duped into pointing the finger at the Fubars by those Dundas guys that are still pissed at them for beating them in court and making them look like a bunch of rubes."

"So we're still at square one without any clues," said Zack.

***

Bud was assigned to respond to a call from an address on South Lincoln Street. Bud knew the elderly rider from his time at St. Olaf, a professor of economics who happened to be the father of Milton Grubbs.

"Where to, Professor Grubbs?" asked Bud.

"Montgomery – the Monty Bar and Hotel," said Colin Grubbs.

"Yes, sir. I'll have to stop and get gas before we go," said Bud. Then he spoke into the microphone, "Seven going to Montgomery, Minnesota."

"Seven to Montgomery, got it." came back the reply. "See you in about an hour."

Stopping at Finney's Gas Station, Bud had his tank filled with 30 cent gasoline while Finney washed his windshield and checked his oil and radiator.

"Everything looks good," said Finney as he

closed the hood on the 1954 Dodge.

Bud and his passenger headed west on Highway 19, through the gently rolling hills, cornfields, and wetlands. Some Northfielders referred to the residents of this area west of Northfield as "bohunks" since it was originally settled by Czech immigrants from Bohemia in the 1870s.

"Going to Kolacky Days?" asked Bud as the smell of freshly cut alfalfa wafted through the cab.

Kolacky Days was an annual festival that began in 1929 to celebrate the residents' Czech heritage. It focused on a sweet pastry that holds portions of fruit, cheese, and spices surrounded by puffy dough named the "kolache," the old Slavonic word meaning circle or wheel. The two-day event drew lots of people into town to devour several versions of this delicacy, watch a parade and fireworks, go to the "Czech Mardi Gras," play sports, race, and, most importantly, drink a lot of beer.

"Yes, I go over every year. Have a lady friend over there. We go around to all the events, eat a lot of kolaches, drink a lot of beer, and have a lot of fun. Of course, I wouldn't want that to get back to the powers that be at St. Olaf. They're kind of stuffy about drinking and most forms of self-indulgence. They don't even allow dancing on campus. Can you believe that in this day and age?"

"Yeah, no PDA is their motto – no public displays of affection. You don't have to worry, I won't rat you out, professor."

"It was nearly 20 years ago that my wife died

and I had to raise my son, Milton, all alone. I guess I wasn't too good at it 'cause he got into a lot of trouble over the years, stealing money, couldn't keep a job, partied a lot, had to bail him out of jail."

"Milt's working as a bartender at the Crow's Nest Bar now, isn't he?" asked Bud.

"He's been there longer than most places he's worked. I wanted him to go to St. Olaf and make something of himself but no, he'd have none of it. He tried Rochester Junior College for one semester and then flunked out. Didn't tell me about it. 'That's not my thing,' he said. He didn't like to read, couldn't stand to study, always relied on his wits to get by. 'I want to enjoy every moment, get out and have fun, take risks, have some adventure in my life,' he said. Well, he had so much fun and adventure he ended up in jail!"

"Oh, that's too bad," said Bud as he looked at his passenger in the rearview mirror. "Couldn't see the larger picture, eh?"

"Hell, no! And it wasn't just once he got thrown in jail. Most of the time it was for being drunk and disorderly but one time he stole money from the guy he worked for. The employer pressed charges and the court wouldn't listen to my pleas for leniency. So he was sentenced to a few days in jail and I thought maybe it might get the message through to him. But it didn't turn out that way."

"What happened?" asked Bud.

"Well, another drunk guy got jailed while he was serving his sentence, a red-haired dude, He decided to have a cigarette and ended up setting his mattress afire. It was in that little cinder-block building down behind the Fire Department and the whole place filled with smoke and suffocated the guy. It was at night, they forgot to turn on the light outside the jail that indicated it was occupied and nobody checked in on them. Milt screamed for help but no one could hear him. He was lucky to get out alive. So then he was even more resentful than before. He hates me and he hates the city."

"Wow! I can see where that would be hard for him to accept. But his own actions landed him there and he was lucky that he survived the fire. He could have taken it as a close call and a warning that he needed to change his ways."

"I had hoped it would but instead he just drank and caroused more and began to hang out with some of the local riff-raff."

"Did you ever try to get some help for him?"

"Yeah, but he refused to talk with anyone. I talked with one of the psychology professors at St. Olaf. He thought I was probably neglectful and overly indulgent and I probably was. 'Course this professor's kid didn't turn out any better than mine – and he was a psychologist for Christ's sake!

"I had a lot to do to prepare for my classes and grade papers. I didn't earn much money in my early years so I had to rely on some less than ideal babysitters. He could easily manipulate some of them because they felt sorry for him and some of the others had their boyfriends over when they were supposed to be watching him, so he felt justified in pushing the limits as far as he could. So that's maybe where he got used to manipulating others and seeing how much he could get away with."

"Do you see him very often now?"

"No, I haven't seen him for two years. He thinks I betrayed him and he won't let me forget it. I don't know what to do – just wait, I guess."

"Yeah, maybe he'll come around when he's older," said Bud unconvincingly.

Traffic was heavy as they came into Montgomery. There were outdoor stands everywhere and people were dressed in costume and paint. The professor gave directions once they got into town, guiding them to the Monty Hotel on First Street.

"That will be $8.00, Mr. Grubbs," said Bud.

"It's been a nice ride," said Mr. Grubbs as he handed Bud a ten-dollar bill. "Keep the change. You're a good listener. I'll ask for you when I call for a ride back to Northfield."

"Thanks," said Bud.

On his way out of town, Bud spotted a display of old, restored, and customized cars and decided to take a look. He marveled at the skill and attention to detail taken by these backyard mechanics. The cool ones were lowered, chopped, and channeled into sleek street rods. Bud's experience at working on cars was driven by economics and had been frustrating, ending up with bruised knuckles and sore, over-stretched muscles. Before getting back into his cab, he bought a dozen kolaches to bring back to the guys at the cab stand.

On the way back, Bud thought about what the professor had said. Must have been hard on him to lose his wife and then have his son fuck up his life and turn against him. I wonder who these guys are that he is associated with. I wonder if he is involved in these robberies? Probably not.

When Bud entered the cab stand he announced, "Bought you guys a present from the Kolacky Capital of the World," as he opened the box of delicacies.

"Wow! I haven't been out there for ages. I love these things," said Tomorrow Thompson.

Drivers, dispatcher, and visitors dove into the kolaches until the box was soon empty. Bud waited until only Zack and Fat were in the office before telling them about his conversation with Professor Grubbs and his suspicions about Milt.

Zack said, "Sounds like a possible to me."

"I've known Colin Grubbs since he came to Northfield and started teaching at St. Olaf," said Fat. "I've given him many rides in the cab and talked with him a lot. I know he wouldn't be involved in anything like this but that kid of his, I don't know. I know he had gotten himself into a lot of trouble in his younger years but I thought he had calmed down since he started working at the Crow's Nest. It's probably nothing but, still, I think I'll mention it to Chief Brandt."

***

Zack had been seeing Becky nearly every night since their *South Pacific* night. They were gradually becoming more comfortable with each other and sharing more about how they appraised different objects and events. Zack could tell they had a different take on several aspects of life. He had a more contemplative or reflective approach to experience while she was more practical and down to earth. Her virtues were readily apparent: realistic, kind, attentive to the needs of others, loyal, respectful of tradition.

He got it that she respected her elders and believed that established procedures and authority persisted because they functioned well. And that, therefore, she would support change only if data could demonstrate its practical benefit. But that made it difficult for her to appreciate people, like him, who valued change just for the novelty of it. And dealing with people who did not revere "facts" to the same degree as she or liked to use their imaginations to spin fanciful visions of the future, could make her erupt into harsh, negative, and extreme reactions. She could become stubborn and inflexible and hurl sarcastic invectives that would hit the mark (and throw a wet blanket on any burgeoning ardor).

Becky complained a lot about people at work not doing what they were supposed to do and their superiors not holding them to account. She didn't like being required to do anything that didn't make sense to her. When her criticisms or suggestions were ignored, she felt unappreciated and resentful and had the urge to leave work in the middle of the day and go shopping or to a movie. But she didn't enact her impulsive urge, instead criticizing herself as irresponsible and reckless for considering it.

I don't know about this, Zack thought as he rode up to Becky's house. We might have some long-term conflicts we can't resolve. Guess I'll see how it plays out. Don't need to decide right now.

Dale was on the porch, having a beer. "What do you say, Zack?" he asked.

"Hi, Dale. Not much to say, how's it going for you, ?"

"Same old shit," said Dale. "But things may change here before long. Maybe I'll get out of the taxicab business and do something else."

"What's that, Dale? What do you have in mind?"

"Oh, I don't know. Just thinking. Maybe I'll get out of town and do something bold – go out west, become a cowboy, join the army, start a business. I like to live on the edge. I want to do something exciting, take on a challenge. I don't want to end up like my dad having to have everything planned a week in advance and scared of the unknown and unexpected."

"So I guess going to Dunwoody and learning a trade isn't up your alley?" asked Zack.

"Good god no!" exclaimed Dale. "That would

drive me bonkers from boredom!"

Hearing Zack's motorcycle, Becky came downstairs and walked onto the porch. "I thought I heard you arrive. Can we take a ride somewhere? I need to get out of the house."

"Sure," said Zack. Let's go. See you, Dale. Good luck with your plans."

"Yeah," said Dale. "I've got plans, alright," he muttered to himself.

Once on the Zundapp, Zack asked, "Where do you want to go?"

"Anyplace away from here," said Becky.

Zack headed over to the park on the east side of the high school, just east of College Street. Parking his motorcycle in the lot next to the new addition to the school, they walked over to a table and bench in the section where he used to play soccer with kids displaced from Latvia, Lithuania, and Estonia due to WWII. He smiled as he recalled the skill of the Europeans in a sport that was newly introduced to the States. His team had kids from all of those countries and they won every game.

"What's happening, Becky? You seem upset," asked Zack.

"I am. Our house has been a madhouse for the last few days. Dale has been talking about leaving home and doing something venturesome in some far-off place. Venturesome, can you believe that? What the hell does he think he is, a secret agent, a pirate? Dad went through the roof. Said his son had no idea of the dangers in the world and would get himself killed. My mother was just completely frazzled. 'My son, my son,' she wailed."

"Doesn't sound to me like he has any ideas worked out yet," said Zack. "Maybe it won't seem so ominous once he looks at how to implement his plan."

"Plan? He's got no plan," said Becky in her most sarcastic tone. "He just wants to go off on one of his crackpot adventures with those goof-ball friends of his."

"Who's he hanging out with?" asked Zack.

"Oh, it's that Milt Grubbs and that stupid Clarence at the gas station and I can't remember who else. They're all a bunch of losers. I can't believe my brother falls for their bullshit. He's got enough of his own."

"Well, he is an adult and it is probably time for him to leave home. Maybe you could get him to start by getting a place of his own."

"I'm worried about him," said Becky. "He is my brother and I don't want him to get into trouble."

7 DEFEATING JESSE JAMES

Harold Grant, proprietor of the electric business next door to the 777 cab office, was out in front of his building, swatting flies that landed on his huge glass display windows. Every time he would make a kill, he would sprinkle the spot with Windex and wipe it off, muttering some vilification of the winged intruder. Laura Baddgor came out of her White Castle next door to see what all the fuss was about and lambasted Harold for being a "silly old coot."

"Go back in your hole-in-the-wall salmonella den, you wicked witch of the downtown eateries!" yelled Harold as he wielded his swatter in her direction.

"Demented old fart! Can't take any advise," said Laura as she stomped back into her cafe.

Tiring of his quixotic endeavor to rid his part of Division Street of pestilence, Harold walked into the cab office.

"How's the War of the Flies going," chuckled Fat.

"Eh! It's a losing battle," acknowledged Harold.

"The little bastards don't seem to learn a damn thing, just like our two-bit politicians!"

"You getting ready for the Defeat of Jesse James Days, Harold?" asked Fat.

"Nah doesn't mean anything to me," said Harold. "I guess I'll grow a beard and look like a bum for a few weeks."

The Defeat of Jesse James Days was started by local merchants as just plain "Jesse James Days" in 1948 in order to promote business activity in the community. Because many people, including Kathrine Wulfsberg the high school social studies and history teacher, objected to the idea that the city should celebrate an outlaw, the "Defeat of'" prefix was added to the name to make it more acceptable to those with a distaste for pecuniary motives.

The event being celebrated was the attempted bank robbery on September 7, 1876 by the combined gangs of Jesse James and Cole Younger. The James brothers were well known by that time and got major billing by newspapers when the event occurred.

They grew up in Clay County along the Missouri River. Their father, Robert, was a college educated hemp farmer and charismatic Revivalist Baptist minister who, hearing stories of the gold fields in California, said he felt a "calling" to go there to minister to the spiritual needs of the miners. Those who knew him speculated that he may have just wanted to get away from his fault-finding wife, Zerelda. Leaving her and their three children behind in Missouri, he headed to the Golden State, only to perish there from cholera. Because of the inheritance laws of the time, Zerelda lost the farm but regained it when she married Dr. Reuben Samuel, whom she totally dominated.

A militia group looking for Frank James dragged and beat young Jesse and had him watch as they strung his stepfather up from a tree until he revealed the whereabouts of Frank. At 16 years of age Jesse joined the bushwhackers where his callousness and brutality were hardened by violent performances that gained him respect among his fellows. He was a true believer in the causes of the South even after its collapse, killed neighbors he saw as enemies, and became famous through the efforts of newspaperman John Newman Edwards who, for reasons of his own, promoted Jesse as a kind of Robin Hood who was reacting to the injustices wrought by the Federals.

As his criminal career developed, Jesse began to play to his imagined Confederate audience and his ego by leaving "press releases" at the scenes of robberies, writing letters to newspapers protesting his innocence, claiming he robbed from the rich and gave to the poor, denouncing the railroads and espousing his Southern political views. By the time of the raid at Northfield, the James brothers were famously implicated in 11 bank robberies and eight holdups of trains, stagecoaches and omnibuses.

Jesse had just turned 29 years of age two days

before the raid, was six feet tall, handsome and slender with piercing blue or hazel eyes. He shared his brother's interest in fine horseflesh, horse racing and playing faro. He was smart, calculating, politically aware, and enamored with the image that he and his newspaper friend had created of him. He was more impetuous, daring and reckless than his brother and was said to be moody with a flair for the dramatic.

Cole Younger was a large man, 6' 4" and heavy set with a dominant voice and a propensity for swearing. His father was wealthy and politically prominent, having been a county court judge and representative in the state legislature. Captain Irvin Walley, commander of the Missouri Militia, imprisoned three of Cole's sisters, some of his cousins and 25 other women on trumped up charges. The building in which they were housed was secretly undermined, causing it to cave in killing or injuring all but three of the prisoners. According to Cole, Walley also murdered Cole's father when he was returning from a trip related to raids on his stable, stage line, and stores and forced Cole's mother to set fire to her own home.

Cole believed he was "born for better things" but due to the murder of his father, the burning-out of his mother and the incarceration of three of his sisters, he developed such hatred and desire for revenge that he was side-tracked from the future he had thought would be his. It was said that he systematically hunted down and killed each of the men responsible for his father's death.

Cole younger was accompanied by brothers Bob and Jim. Friendly and soft-spoken Bob Younger was the most handsome of the outlaw band and, at 23 years of age, was the youngest of the Younger clan. Jesse James mentored him, to the apparent consternation of Cole. Cole claimed that Bob had dropped out of William and Mary College because he was harassed for being Cole's brother, but it is likely that this was just another self-aggrandizing tale Cole was prone to relate.

Jim Younger, quiet and acquiescent, was 28 years old and, like Bob, seemed to resent the constant interference in the conduct of his life by his strapping older brother Cole. The Northfield Raid may have been his first robbery. He had been regularly working a respectable job in California until Cole sent him a telegram asking him to come home because Bob needed him.

The First National Bank of Northfield, which opened in 1873 with a capitalization of $50,000 from local investors, was the successor to the Bank of Northfield, which had been in operation for eight years. It was located in the 400 block of Division Street in the back of a large roughhewn limestone building erected by Hiram Scriver, Northfield's first significant merchant and first mayor. The front face of the building was on Mill Square (now called Bridge Square) and housed Scriver's dry goods store and a general store operated by Lee and Hitchcock. Dentist D. J. Whiting had his office on the second floor at the end of a wooden staircase that went up the outside of the building.

Cole Younger claimed he had learned that "Beast Butler" and his son-in-law Adelbert Ames had $75,000 deposited in the bank, which he believed was stolen or swindled from Southerners, and they sought to extract some revenge. Benjamin F. Butler, an influential congressman and former Major General, was vilified as "Beast Butler" for his callous administration of Union-occupied New Orleans during the Civil War. He was a political wheeler-dealer who somehow amassed an estate of $7,000,000 though he had a penniless beginning.

After the war, Interim Secretary of War U. S. Grant under President Johnson appointed Adelbert (or "Del," as he was called) Ames Provisional Governor of Mississippi under reconstruction. He was elected senator in 1870 by a unanimous vote of Republicans in the Senate and 72 in the House and in 1873 he was elected governor of Mississippi in his own right.

In his work during reconstruction in Mississippi Del made valiant efforts to make the program work by supporting freed slaves for pubic office, developing integrated free public schools, and running a frugal government. His efforts were undermined by a widespread conspiracy of Democrats who resented loss of their economic basis for a good life, and carried the Civil War on "by other means," which included murder of black activists and terrorism of black voters and anyone who supported them.

Disillusioned with lack of support from Washington, Ames came to Northfield on May 11, 1876 to begin work in the mill with his brother and father. His wife, Blanche, and two children continued to live in Massachusetts with her parents

Bob Younger said that the gang selected the Northfield bank because they had learned that Ames had money in the bank and "one of the boys had a spite against him."

Jesse James probably believed that a successful raid on a symbol of northern dominance could provide some revenge against the Unionists who had disrupted his way of life before the Emancipation Proclamation and subjected his family to various indignities. He thought he might be able to inspire like-minded individuals in southern states to take similar action and he could show carpetbaggers there was no place they could feel safe from Southerners seeking to get even. Of course, he would be able to polish his ego on a national stage and there was, alas, the possibly of gaining a lot of loot.

On September 7, after a meal at Jeft's diner next to the railroad station and a final inspection of the town, including checking to see what kind of weaponry was for sale, the gang reassembled on the west side and voted to make the raid. They separated into three groups as they rode into town: a forward set of three that was to enter the bank as soon as another set of two riders crossed the iron bridge over the Cannon River, and a third set of three a quarter mile behind that was to wait at the bridge and give the rebel yell and fire pistols in the air to scare off any meddling townspeople.

The first three bandits entered the bank, jumped the counter, and began demanding to know which of the three bank employees was the cashier. All of them truthfully replied that they weren't since the official cashier was George M. Phillips, who was out of town. The outlaws perceived Joseph Lee Heywood to be the oldest, believed he must be the cashier and demanded that he open the safe. Although the safe was already open, Heywood demurred, saying that it was on a time lock and could not be opened at that time.

One desperado entered the door to the vault and Heywood tried to close the door on him, only to be seized by the other two villains and have a knife drawn across his throat and a pistol fired near his head with threats to his life and further demands to open the safe. At some point Heywood yelled "Murder! Murder! Murder!" whereupon Frank James clunked him on the head with his revolver, causing him to fall, dizzy and partly unconscious.

Meanwhile, outside the bank, several citizens became suspicious when the eight riders appeared. J. S. Allen, who operated a hardware store on the square, went to the bank to investigate and was manhandled and threatened by one of the bandits. That tipped off all the towns people that were watching and the alarm went out "Robbers at the bank!" As outlaws rode up and down the street firing into store windows and yelling at citizens to stay out of the way, Elias Stacey fired a load of birdshot into the face of a robber, knocking him from his horse but causing no disabling injury.

As Cole Younger pleaded with the members of the gang still in the bank "For god's sake come out; they are shooting us all to pieces," the bank's bookkeeper made a run for it through the blinds and out the back door. A bandit was on his trail and shot him in the shoulder but he managed to keep going to a doctor's office nearby, where he received treatment. One of the gang turned as he was leaving and shot the defiant Heywood in the head, killing him.

Law enforcement officers from Minneapolis and St. Paul, Faribault and various other communities in southern Minnesota and some military units joined in the chase and numerous posses were formed. A former general was called upon to coordinate some of the posses although there were many pursuing groups that acted independently and often foolishly.

The bank, the governor and the railway companies offered large rewards for capture of the outlaws dead or alive which eventually helped to swell the ranks of the pursuers to over a thousand. Railroads brought in would-be captors from far and wide and ferried them out to where the latest rumors located the villains. There were lots of erroneous sightings, men who were derelict in their assignments, and many lost opportunities.

Minneapolis detective Mike Hoy competed with St. Paul detective John Bresett for the glory of capturing the famous outlaws but neither of them succeeded. Although the chase in southern Minnesota often seemed like a circus, roads, railroads, bridges and fords were staked out effectively enough to make it difficult for the brigands freely to navigate the countryside and to effect their escape.

The bandits were finally cornered in an area of heavy underbrush known as the Hanska Slough and seven volunteers marching in a line four paces apart flushed the gang out of the thickets. After a brief but intense gun fight at a range of 30 feet, one was killed, one was shot in the chest, one was shot five times, and Cole Younger was hit 11 times.

The bleeding prisoners were piled into a wagon and taken to the nearby Flanders House. As the hotel filled with reporters, photographers and the curious, the men's wounds were treated, their wet and tattered clothes replaced and they were fed. There was a serious threat of a lynching but law enforcement officers and local citizens prevented any implementation of the threat.

***

"I've never been a beard-grower," said Fat Lloyd. "I leave that talent to Tiny Johnson. His beard is already longer than anyone else's in town, save for old Bill Schilling's."

For the 1948 celebration, the lamp posts and buildings were decorated with bunting and store windows displayed antiques. There was just one re-enactment of the raid, held at the corner of the Scriver Building where the old wooden paving blocks of Bridge Square met with the concrete of Division Street. Subsequent celebrations moved the site to the old 112 Taxi Office adorned with a cardboard sign that read "Bank."

The celebrations became more elaborate and longer as the years passed with parades, square dancing, beard-growing contests, best looking outlaw contests, tractor pulls, gifts and awards, a carnival on the west side of the river next to the Malt-O-Meal plant, and various parties.

"What with all the money that has been put into this thing by us taxpayers, I just hope the festival is a hit this year," said Harold . "And pray that we don't get a lot of rain and the river floods. That could be a disaster!"

"For sure," retorted Fat.

"Guess I'll go over and make up with Laura," said Harold. "She's a cantankerous old biddy but I love her spunk."

8 PRACTICE MAKES PERFECT

Milt called a late afternoon meeting of his gang at the park adjacent to Odd Fellows home, at Lincoln and Forest Avenue. Fittingly, this was the same vicinity where the James-Younger Gang rendez-voused before attempting to rob the First National Bank on September 7, 1876. They, too, must have appreciated the little grove where gentle breezes flowed through the oaks and maples that provided abundant shade from the summer sun. Howard brought two six-packs of beer and Billy brought some potato chips from his cafe. Everyone sat around an A-framed wooden picnic table with at-tached benches and opened a brew from Bub's Brewing Company in Faribault.

"Ahh," said Clarence as he took a swig. "Damn good beer at $4.00 a case."

"Yeah, you betcha!" everyone agreed.

Standing, Milt began, "Now, I think last time we decided it would be impossible to gain entrance through the roof – too noisy or too dangerous. Howard, how did you assess that front door?"

"Well, it's just a double door with brass plating. It would probably be easiest to cut the latch with an acetylene torch. Using a saw on it would be pretty noisy."

"How long do you think it would take?"

"Probably about five to ten minutes. And there would be sparks flying and lighting up the area."

"Don't like that unless we could be sure that Officer Tasty or some busybody wouldn't be driving by during that time," said Milt.

"We could call in an anonymous request for police assistance up on the far side of town before starting the torch. Keep them occupied while we are getting in," said Billy. "Or I could station myself on Bridge Square and honk my horn if I saw them coming."

"Eh...," scowled Milt.

"The windows on the street side are all hooked up to the alarm system, so we can't just break one and go in," said Howard. "And there is no way we can get to the wires for the alarm. They all are inside the wall."

"What about the safe and the vault?" asked Milt.

"The safe is a no-go, as far as I can tell," said Howard. "It weighs 5000 pounds and is on a double time lock. To have time enough to cut into it, we'd have to take it with us, and to do that we'd have to have some kind of hoist to lift it into a truck, assuming we could even get it out of the building."

"And the vault?"

"We could probably cut the door open with a torch but it might take quite a bit of time, said Howard. We could use a canvas drop cloth to hide the sparks but it would have to be a ways back from the vault door or we could start it on fire. Wouldn't that be a hell of a note! I'm estimating we'd have to allow a couple of hours to pull that off."

"Uffda! The gods, they are conspiring against us. Give me another beer, Billy," said Milt. He paced back and forth near the table.

"It's getting to sound to me like a nighttime operation would be a goddamn nightmare. Too many obstacles to overcome, too much equipment to haul around, too many things could go wrong. Looks like we'll have to go in during broad daylight when the doors are open and everyone is at their posts - just like our predecessors did 80 some years ago!"

"Holy shit!" exclaimed Billy. "They're going to be able to identify us for sure."

"Not if we wear wigs and face masks," said Milt.

"Come on, you guys, have some balls here," said Clarence. "We can do this. Give Milt a chance to lay out a plan."

"Let's take a look at what we know," said the analytical Howard. "We know the tellers and the cashier come in at 8:00 am. And they stay until five – two hours after closing the front door. The president straggles in some time in the late morn-ing and the customers drop in any time, but the busiest times are 11:00 in the morning and 2:00 in the afternoon. The armored car can show up any time on any day – they just call for it when they need it. I would think the best time for the heist would be just before closing, at 3:00. Or we could do it as soon as they open up in the morning, but we wouldn't want to get too close to 11:00 or we'd have a bunch of customers clamoring at the door."

Milt paced some more and sat his beer on the table. "Dale, did you learn anything from your sister?" he asked.

"Yeah," Dale responded. "The vault is open the whole day and the safe gets opened when something gets deposited or withdrawn, but it's locked otherwise."

"Who has the combination to the safe?" asked Milt.

"The cashier. He also has the master key to all the safe deposit boxes."

"So we will want to have someone get to the cashier right away before he can sound the alarm or dispose of the master key," said Howard. "Maybe we need some leverage to get him to cough up the combination if he gets resistive as old Heywood did. Like maybe a phone call to someone holding a relative hostage?"

"Good idea," said Milt. "We might not have to have an actual hostage. Just be able to convince him that we do. Like we park a car across the street from his house and have the cashier make a phone call to his wife or daughter or whoever and ask them to look outside and see if a particular kind of car is parked outside. Then we tell the cashier that bad people in that car are going to harm his relative if he doesn't give us the combination."

"Sounds like a winner to me," said Clarence.

"I'm not so sure," said Dale. "What if they go out and check out the car?"

"We'd make sure the cashier would discourage them from doing that by telling him, if they came close to the car, they would get killed," said Milt. "He would have no way of knowing that we were bluffing."

"We would be bluffing, wouldn't we?" asked Billy.

"Yeah. Yeah. Don't worry about it, Billy," said Milt. "We don't want to hurt anybody. Well, maybe rough them up some, but not kill them. We don't want the whole damn state to be looking for us for a murder rap."

"For a backup, we could threaten the lives of the tellers or any customers in the bank," said Dale. "Those bankers don't like bad publicity – it wouldn't look good if the bank cared more about their money than its employees or its customers."

"And, Dale, what did your sister say about how much money each of the tellers has and what is in the safe-deposit boxes?"

"They start with about $1000 each in their tills and that gets replenished from the safe whenever necessary. So let's say there is a total of about $3000 in cash in the teller windows. Safe deposit boxes can contain anything that the customer considers of value – important papers, mementos, jewelry, stocks, and bonds. The bank kind of discourages people putting cash in there but there is no rule against it, so there may be cash in some of them, maybe cash the owner doesn't want anyone else to know about."

"What are we looking at for cash in the safe?" asked Milt.

"Probably about $20,000 in the safe," said Dale. "And the safe is in the vault. Cash is rotated from the tellers to the vault fairly regularly as the bank takes old bills out of circulation and puts new bills into circulation. If you get some badly worn bills from a teller, that means they have had a heavy cash day."

"So if we maxed out on this caper, we'd get about $6000 each," said Milt. "Not exactly a Great Brinks Robbery but you could buy 3 new cars or 2 if you got real fancy."

Raising his hand, Clarence said, "And it wouldn't be the end of our careers, either, if we get good at it."

"Don't you think we need a distraction?" asked Howard. "A good one is coming up here in a few months – the Defeat of Jesse James Days. We could do it when they are doing the re-enactment when everyone is over on Division Street and people are shooting off guns and loudspeakers are blaring. There would be more people in town but that just adds to the confusion and besides, the bank might have more money to handle the onslaught of visitors."

"Good thinking, Howard," said Milt.

"We're going to need everything going in our favor to pull this off," said Dale as he polished off his second beer. "How are we going to get away? The bridge will be blocked off during the re-enactment. They'll have barricades at Third and Water and up at Division and Fourth to keep the tourists from driving into the friggin horses and re-enactors."

"We can tie up all the employees and customers but after a couple of hours someone is going to come looking for them when they don't show up for dinner or whatever," observed Dale.

"Once it's known there was a robbery, all the highways will be full of state police and sheriffs officers within a few minutes. If we are on the road, our goose is cooked," worried Billy.

"How about we go down the river?" asked Clarence.

Milt replied, incredulously, "The river? Are you kidding me? The river!"

"Just a minute," said Howard. "The big guy may have something there. No one would expect us to be on the river. They'd be looking on all the highways and streets. We could have a couple of rubber rafts with outboards on the back that we could start after we drifted away from the bank – a silent getaway."

"How would we get into them?" asked Dale.

"We could go out the basement windows and slide

down on a rope," offered Clarence. " 'Course then we'd have to have someone in one of the boats and he'd have to keep them from floating away."

"We could sneak in a day or two before and put an eye-bolt into the wall under the bank," suggested Dale. "Then, on the day of the robbery, our guy could drive one boat pulling the other and attach it to the bolt. The guys in the bank could then bring down our take and lower it to the boats by rope and then slide down themselves."

"Whoa, whoa!" exclaimed Milt, swinging both arms in the air. "This is getting too damn complicated. We'd probably end up swimming to Lake Byllesby! How about we think about going out the front door, making a right, and going down to the alley next to Zanmiller's Sheet Metal Shop and getting down to the river from there. It would only take about three minutes. We could have the boats tied up there, out of sight from Bridge Square and the re-enactment watchers. Maybe we could have Des watch them until we got there." Laughing, he said, "She always likes to please. Then we could silently float away and start our motors when we reach the Second Street Bridge."

"How much stuff are we going to be carrying?" asked Billy. "We might need some kind of cart handy to push down the street."

"Too conspicuous," said Milt. "We can't go down the street in a pack either or shop and cafe owners on Water Street, those that aren't up on the Square, would wonder what was up. Best we leave the bank one or two at a time, a few minutes apart. Carry a shopping bag with 'Defeat of Jesse James Days' displayed on it. Or 'Perman's' or 'Jacobson's' – the kind of bags everyone carries around here."

"We can store some cars down river the night before at the old Travelers Park or down in Waterford or even further down," said Howard. "Even better, if we could boat all the way down to Lake Byllesby and stay for a few days at a cabin there. Let things blow over. Does anyone know of one that won't be occupied this time of year?"

"I can check that out, said Billy. "I have a friend that has a little house down there. He'll know who's closed up for the season and what places are occupied. I'll get back to you on that."

"Great," said Milt. "Now we need to figure out our ground game for entering the bank."

"This is the part that scares the hell out of me," said Billy as he opened up a new beer.

"Our main tools are fear and intimidation," said Milt. "Just like with the college students. We want to scare the employees into submission and obedience so they follow our commands without thinking of doing anything else. That means we need to carry guns and big knives and wield them like we mean business. We want to avoid hurting anyone very badly if we can, but if someone makes a move to alert anyone on the outside, they need to be stopped one way or another."

Billy fixed his gaze on Milt for a few seconds and then looked away, thinking that he didn't like the sound of that. Does that mean we shoot someone who tries to get away?

"I suggest we wear cowboy outfits with big hats and bandannas so we kind of blend in with the tourists and locals dressed up for the festivities," said Howard. "That way we can get through the door and get to the cashier before they realize they are being robbed. The last guy in locks the door."

Milt adds, "These are the roles I propose for each of us once we get in the bank. Clarence grabs the cashier and pulls him and his master key out of his office, Dale gets behind the teller windows so none of them can press any kind of hidden alarm button, and Howard and I keep guns on all of them. Once we have them under control, Billy ties up the tellers and Clarence gets the cashier to a phone where we have him ring up his wife and tell her to look outside for a green panel truck or whatever – we'll have to steal one. Once he agrees to turn over the combination, Billy ties him up too, and Howard opens the safe while Clarence and I open up the safe-deposit boxes and grab whatever looks valuable and is the kind of stuff we can get rid of. We throw everything into shopping bags and leave the bank about one minute apart. Does anyone have a problem with any of that?"

"Do you really think we can pull this off?" asked Dale with his usual skepticism.

"Come on Dale, you're always the wet blanket every time we plan a job," said Clarence. "Give Milt some credit. Give all of us some credit, for Christ's sake!"

"I'd just feel a little better about it if we could have a trial run somehow," said Dale.

"How about we go out to the old Guptdahl place. It's vacant and we can arrange stuff like the inside of the bank and our escape route. Then we can go through the motions and work out any kinks in our plan," suggested Howard. "We'll need to pace off the distance from the front of the bank to Zanmillers and then down to the river."

"I can do that, said Billy. "I'm down in that area all day and can just take a couple of my breaks to walk the distances. I can pretend I'm making a sketch."

"Good," said Milt. "I'll go over and put something in my safe deposit box and surreptitiously pace off some distances on the inside."

***

The trail up to the old Guptdahl farmhouse from the main road was little more than a path through the wild grass with two ruts worn by the occasional taxi cab taking the former inhabitants to town to sell their berries and vegetables. Since their demise, the premises had deteriorated due to weather and the pillaging of teenagers proving to themselves that they could affect something, even if it was inanimate. Part of the roof was missing and most of the paned windows had been broken but some remained, albeit with bullet holes or the spidery cracks emanating from BB impacts.

The gang arrived in two cars, separated in time by fifteen minutes. No one detected any snoops lurking about on their ride up the knoll but they still felt uneasy about being in alien territory. The members strolled around the house, trying to imagine how it might substitute for the State Bank. Billy paced off a distance about 275 feet, meant to be equivalent to the distance from the State Bank to Zanmiller's Sheet Metal Shop. That put him well past the old garden and near the tree line of the clearing surrounding the house. He then walked along the trees for about 80 feet to represent the distance from Zanmiller's to the riverfront.

"I'm at the river, ready to get into the raft" he yelled.

Almost in unison, everyone else yelled, "What?" Billy tried again but soon realized all the others were laughing. They knew what he meant and he started to laugh too.

As he got within voice range, he said, "If we walk at three miles an hour, it should take us no more than one and a half or two minutes to get to the boats."

"That's acceptable," said Milt. "Now let's make the inside of the house look like the inside of the bank."

The screen door had been partly torn loose from the door frame, so Milt tore it away completely to reveal a frame-panel door that still worked. He walked in and the others soon joined him to gape at the remnants of the former occupants' possessions. Four straight-backed chairs around an oak trestle table marred by veneer peeling from the base; rusting pans in the sink with chipped porcelain; old newspapers used for insulation in the walls; stacks of wooden pint berry containers; a pot-belly iron stove. After letting his men briefly wonder about the lives that might have been led there, Milt broke the spell of the past by focusing on the purpose for which they came.

"OK, let's set up this bank," said Milt. "Put that table over against the wall next to the door. That will be the customer alcove."

Clarence and Dale moved the table.

"Now, put four of those chairs in a row to the right of the door, said Milt. "The first one will represent where the cashier's office is and the next three will be the tellers' cages. The stove can stay where it is as the center customer service table. We'll use that bedroom over there as the boardroom of the bank."

Howard and Billy each took two chairs and arranged them in a semi-circle along the right and rear walls.

"Separate those chairs a little more. That's it," said Milt as the men followed his orders.

They all stepped back toward the door, trying to let their imaginations transform the arranged furniture into an image of the inside of the bank. Grabbing an old pillow, Milt placed it in the first chair.

"There. That's the cashier. Now, Clarence, you

go over to the door and rush in as fast as you can and grab the cashier and threaten him with your knife. I think a knife in your face is scarier than a gun. Using the gun involves a yes or no decision and likely will end up with someone dead. But a knife is more unpredictable and can inflict various degrees of injury, even if it is just a mistake. So rush in there, wave your big knife around so he can see it, grab the cashier and hold the blade up close to his face, demanding the combination to the safe and the master key for the safe deposit boxes."

Clarence went to the door and turned around, facing the inside of the room. He smiled at the others, a bit self-conscious in being on stage. But Milt's stern glare focused his attention on his performance. Rushing toward the first chair, he made the distance in just three steps, grabbed the pillow in his left hand while drawing his knife up to it with his right.

"All right you little asshole, I want two things from you: the combination to the safe and the master key to the safe-deposit boxes. Don't give me any shit or I'll carve you up like I would a T-bone steak!"

"Bravo," hailed Milt and everyone gave Clarence a round of applause. Clarence bowed and doffed his cap.

"Next, I want Dale to rush in behind the teller windows, scare the shit out of the tellers and march them into the board room. At the same time, Howard runs over to the vault and makes sure it stays open while Billy and I come out in front and keep our guns on everybody."

Dale ran over behind the three chairs waving a pistol and proclaimed, "This here is a bank robbery, girls. Now I want you all to march into that boardroom over there and sit on the floor. Give me any back-talk and I'll have to shoot your tits off!" Then he followed the imaginary tellers into the bedroom.

Director Milt instructed, "Billy, you run in there and tie up the tellers' hands behind their backs and then their ankles. Then come back to the vault area."

Billy went through the motions of pretending to do so.

"At this point, if we are lucky, we'll have the combination to the safe and the master key for the safe-deposit boxes," said Milt. "If the cashier is stupid, like Heywood, we'll have to convince him that his family will be beaten up or killed if he doesn't comply. We'll run that scenario after we play out this easier one."

Howard continued the description of the plot, walking it through as he provided the narrative. "So I go over to Clarence and get the combination to the safe, then walk into the vault and dial the combination. Billy takes the cashier into the boardroom and ties him up. I open the safe and put all the folding money into four to six shopping bags. What if there are other valuables in there, like gold bars or coins?"

"Yeah, we can get rid of gold and coins but if there is a lot of it, make sure it gets distributed into different bags so it doesn't fall through or be too heavy for one person to carry," said Milt. "If there are any papers in there, forget about them unless you know what they are and know we can get rid of them for cash."

Milt took up the directing again. "Clarence, you come over and start opening all the safe-deposit boxes. Just turn the key then move on to the next one. I'll come along behind you and open them up. If there's anything inside that we can use, I'll put it in the other bags. If not, I'll just close the box again."

"I think it's time to blow this joint," exclaimed Billy.

"About that time," said Milt. "Before we go out that door we want to stop and make sure we have everything we want to take with us and don't leave anything behind that might identify us."

"For sure," said Dale. "We want to get away clean. I don't want to have a record. I want to be able to come back and see my family. So, yeah, let's not mess this up!"

"OK," said Milt. "Clarence and Billy go out the door together first carrying two bags each. Walk normally and don't be looking over your shoulder all the time. Put your masks down around your necks so you don't draw attention to yourself. Remember, we want to look like locals or tourists enjoying the festivities. If you run into someone you know, greet them and stop and chat a little. But remember we only have a few seconds to waste time. Divert their attention to something going on at the Square. Tell them you'll call them later if they want to bend your ear too long. OK, go ahead. I'll time you."

Clarence and Billy sauntered down toward the tree line and to the make-believe boats, pretending to talk with imaginary acquaintances as they traversed the 120 yards to the banks of the Cannon River. Milt clocked them at just over two minutes.

"OK, now Dale and Howard go out, each carrying two bags. You guys do the same thing. Act normal and nonchalant." Milt clocked the more business-like couple at less than two minutes.

"After two minutes more, I'll join the last two with one or two bags and lock the door behind me. When the first two arrive at the boats, start floating off immediately. Don't start the motor until you get past the Second Street bridge. I'll join the second two at the boats and we'll do the same. I don't think this will happen but if, for some reason, I don't get there after you wait two minutes, take off without me."

"What could keep you from getting there?" asked Billy.

"I'm well known in that part of town," said Milt. "I might have to go have a cup of coffee with someone or listen to some sad tale from one of the guys that frequent the bar. Just to avoid arousing suspicion I might have to spend some time with them. I can talk my way out of it but it might take a while. I'll catch up later if that happens."

The gang had a couple more run-throughs of the scheme. Mostly it went without a hitch except for the times that Clarence accidentally cut off the head of the cashier and Billy goofed around pretending he had his hands under the skirts of the tellers, fondling their private parts.

"What about the boats?" asked Howard. "Where are we going to get the boats?"

"I got that covered," said Milt. "Hughes & Heckler sells those little nine-foot Zodiacs. They have about half a dozen stored in a shack next to their LP gas storage tank. All we have to do is sneak in some night and cart them off. Then we need to pick up a couple of five horsepower outboard motors and we're in business. There are lots of Johnson and Evinrudes sitting in back yards all over town so we shouldn't have a problem there. 'Course we'll have to try them out so we know we can rely on them."

9 YTTERBOE IS DEAD

"Bud, it's your turn to take Rossing to the airport today," said Fat. "Make sure you're gassed up and ready to go by 1:00."

"Probably going to Chicago again," said Bud. "He consults at Argonne National Laboratories there. That's where he went last time."

Bud drove up to the house across the street from Northfield High School. Soon, Professor Rossing came down the walkway with a suitcase and large briefcase. He was a tall, stocky man of 30 years, slightly hunched over from when he did farm work in the small Minnesota town of his origin where his father was a minister. Bud put the suitcase in the trunk while the professor took the briefcase into the back seat of the cab where he could work on his project while on the way to the airport.

Bud knew his passenger from when he went to St. Olaf and took courses in nuclear physics and electronics from him. He remembered Rossing taking a busload of physics students up to McAllister College to see Niels Bohr, an icon in early nuclear physics, give a lecture on the value of studying the one-electron atom. Bud still recalled feeling like he was doing "real" nuclear physics when Rossing had students separate U235 from U238 in one class, just as Rossing had done at Iowa State where he did his graduate work.

The professor remembered Bud because he was the only student in one of his quantum mechanics classes who correctly answered a test question involving operator equations. When that was reveled in class, Bud was embarrassed to be the center of attention for all those who didn't solve the problem. He explained his brief moment of glory by saying that he got the answer correct simply because he followed the rules for that type of equation. Rossing liked that modest answer and thought it reflected his prowess in teaching.

"Going to Argonne again, professor?" Bud asked as they got on their way up Highway 3.

"Yes. They seem to like me there. When I worked for Remington Rand before I came to St. Olaf, I was working on applied magnetism, primarily magnetic films for computer memory. They wanted to get away from all those ferrite cores and bundles of wires running everywhere in three dimensions. We were working toward miniaturization by making very thin films. "

"You worked for Remington Rand? I remember going up there when I was in high school," said Bud. "Our geometry teacher, Paul Jorgenson, arranged for a trip to view their new Univac computer. We even had to get fingerprinted by the FBI to take the tour. The machine was huge – nearly 400 square feet of floor space. They showed us the printed circuits they were developing and using. There were a lot of technicians tending to the needs of the machine with doors off here and there where you could look in and see a mass of wires and boards connected with little metal snaps."

"They've moved on to a new version now. I was still doing spin-wave resonance in magnetic thin films when I came to St. Olaf, but I decided to start a program in acoustics. I like music and I have played with orchestras at times. I started teaching the physics of music at St. Olaf, which is a great place for it given their famous choirs and orchestras."

"Indeed. Do you think you will continue with those interests?"

"Oh, yes. I want to figure out the physics of all the musical instruments, such as the vibrations that bells make. Musical sounds as we hear them depend on both the wavelength patterns of the instrument and our physical and mental mechanisms for deciphering those vibrations. So this area of research should actually be called psychoacoustics," opined Rossing.

"That's very interesting. I have become fascinated with the research going on in psycholinguistics – how we decipher vocal and written language to communicate. Maybe psycholinguistics should be considered a part of psychoacoustics?" Bud ventured.

"Perhaps so," said the professor. "How did you get interested in psycholinguistics? I thought you were in the pre-engineering program at St. Olaf. Why didn't you continue with that?"

"I was but then I took a year off to save money for my second two years of college and I decided to transfer to the University because the tuition is only $45 per quarter, no matter how many courses you take. I liked nuclear physics a lot but couldn't imagine myself being a teacher – I'm more of a doer, I think - and my involvement in the pre-engineering program was just because that was what all my friends were into in high school. Then I started to read a lot of psychology and psychiatry books and got interested in how the mind works."

"You mean like Freud and Jung and psychoanalysis?"

"Yeah, but I leaned more toward the neo-Freudians – people like Eric Fromm, Karen Horney, and Harry Stack Sullivan. They focused more on relationships, culture, and social learning as determinants of thinking patterns and behavior. I found that interesting and I wanted to learn more, so when I transferred to UMN, I changed my major to psychology with a minor in sociology."

"Do you have in mind becoming a practitioner, a clinician?"

"I don't know. I can imagine myself doing what they do – listening to and talking with patients or clients, trying to help them think through problems and move on in life. So I am attracted to that kind of role. There are also a lot of jobs available right now in the practical application of psychology, more than for academic jobs. It has that going for it."

"So what was the University like for you?"

"Well, on orientation, they assembled all of us transfer students together and said we could expect to do less well than we had done in our little private schools. For me, it turned out to be just the opposite. I did very well and received A's in most of my courses. I think I had become more serious about studying too – became more organized, took copious notes, gave up some of my bad habits like not memorizing anything that I could derive from basic principles."

"What was wrong with that?" asked Rossing.

"It took too much time when I was taking tests. I took calculus from Clarence Carlson. Do you know him?"

"Yes, a brilliant man and a good teacher."

"Right. He used to put all these equations on the blackboards as fast as he could write and by the end of the hour, he'd have all the blackboards on three sides of the room covered. To continue he'd have to erase with one hand while he wrote with the other."

"Yes, I heard tales about that," Rossing chuckled, "and about his passion for his subject matter."

"When he would give a test, at first I could get all the answers correct by just going back to basics and deriving everything that was needed.

But as the course went along and I didn't memorize part-solutions and had to derive them to solve the problem presented, I'd run out of time and the test would be over. So when I transferred to the U and changed my major, I started memorizing everything and got pretty good at it, figuring out ways to make it more efficient and less boring. And I was rewarded with good grades. I think that is one of the things that got me interested in learning theory. I thought that if we figured out how people learned the concepts and habits they do, that would be the solution to a lot of problems facing humanity."

"Like mental health problems, how to change attitudes and beliefs, and how to teach or learn things more rapidly?" suggested Rossing.

"Exactly! The University of Minnesota is a bastion of learning theory, partly a legacy of B.F. Skinner who used to teach there. One of my professors, Kenneth MacCorquodale, has carried on his tradition and has a course called 'Verbal Behavior.' I took that course and was blown away by the detail with which he analyzed sequences and peculiarities of speech and even interactions between speakers using what he called the interaction paradigm."

Bud was impressed by MacCorquodale, whom he would again encounter in later years, and could even now visualize him giving lectures in a second-floor auditorium at the University. The notes for his lectures were organized on 5 by 8-inch cards that he would place on the counter that spanned the room, but he would only occasionally refer to them as he filled every second of the allotted time with sophisticated and sometimes witty discourse on language as it is used. Everyone said he was "eloquent" and, indeed, he spoke with what sounded like a slight British accent and presented himself like Arthur Treacher, an actor known for playing erudite British menservants or valets. MacCorquodale was a disciple of Skinner and spent his whole career at UMN, even living in an apartment on campus. All the students assumed he was of British descent but he actually grew up in the small town of Olivia, Minnesota two hours west of Minneapolis.

"First impressions can change as you learn more about a subject area. It has for me in physics," Rossing added.

"Yeah, as I read more about it, I am seeing the limitations of that approach. For example, there is a linguist named Noam Chomsky who claims the Skinnerian analysis doesn't explain grammatical constructions or the frequency of different errors in speaking or the fact that nerve impulses do not travel fast enough to explain certain kinds of patterned speech or even skilled movements. A young student of language, Eric Lenneberg, has proposed that the structure of the human brain is predisposed to acquire verbal means of communication. And Charles Osgood, the Semantic Differential guy, is now working on something he calls 'synfax,' or the syntactical facilitation of learning. So there's still a lot to be discovered about language and language learning."

"I can see that you are very excited about this area of study," said Rossing. I work at a more elemental level than that but there are areas of convergence. For example, there is probably a syntax in musical expressions as well as in language."

"Makes sense to me," said Bud.

They were now turning off on Highway 55 going toward the mile-long Mendota Bridge over the Minnesota River.

'Psychology is a young science," said the professor. "You would do well to go into it and get in on the ground floor, so to speak. It has worked well for me to just follow my interests no matter what happens to be the popular thing to do. You have to keep alert to opportunities to expand your knowledge and capabilities. Like, for me, Argonne has a very attractive program where you can work in the summers and part-time during the school year. I have been able to do some extremely interesting work on magnetic levitation for high-speed rail transportation."

"Wow! I bet that is fun to work on. I have applied to graduate school at several universities," said Bud. "I don't know if I'll get admitted and I'll only have money enough for about one semester if I do. But, at least I'll get a chance to see if I like it and maybe I'll be able to get a job to keep me going."

"I'm sure you will get in someplace. When you

do, try to get a tuition scholarship, and maybe you can get a teaching or research assistantship. That's how I got through. Maybe you will have to decide between basic science research and practical application or you might be able to find some way to combine them."

The rest of the trip was made in silence as the professor turned to prepare for his duties at Argonne. Bud pulled up in front of the main terminal at Wold-Chamberlain Field and opened the trunk to retrieve the professor's suitcase. As Rossing handed him the $12.50 fare, Bud thanked him for his advice regarding school as well as the fare and Rossing commented, "It was a pleasure talking with you about your interests in psychology. Keep at it. I'm sure you will succeed."

Bud was buoyed by the vote of confidence from the professor and, on his way back to Northfield, reflected on the different attractions and repulsions of working in basic science as opposed to applied science. Finally, he thought, what the hell, I don't have to make that decision yet. I just need to see how far $800 is going to take me and find some way to support myself once that is gone. Throughout his college career, Bud had been focused on learning the course material. He had never thought it possible that he might qualify for financial assistance or an assistantship position and had never talked with anyone about how to go about it. Now he knew there were options available other than simply working at some hum-drum job and saving money.

When Bud got close to town, he called in "Seven is in Waterford."

"Roger that, Seven," replied Fat. "When you get into town, go down to Fifth Street and come back on Washington and park up there across from the library. We've got kind of a situation going on down here."

"Situation? What the hell's going on?"

"It's complicated. There are people all over the place. I'll tell you when you get here."

Curiosity aroused, Bud gawked at the college students streaming down St. Olaf Avenue onto Water Street and cutting across on the Second Street Bridge, headed for the center of town. As he went east on Fifth Street crossing Division, he glanced down toward Bridge Square and saw what seemed like hundreds of people milling around, some carrying signs. Leaving his cab on Washington so he could get away if needed, he trudged down Third Street to Division which was seething with college students, both Oles and Carls, churning about, yelling and screaming for Percy Morris to come out and face the crowd.

Fat was out in front of the cab stand, chatting with Bob Sletten, Assistant Chief of Police, along with a state trooper. The police squad car was parked in front of City Hall and some of the students were rocking it back and forth in an attempt to turn it over. Failing in that effort, they resorted to letting the air out of its tires.

"Jesus Christ," exclaimed Bud. "What the Sam Hill is going on. This looks like a fucking riot!"

"Well," explained Fat, "it all started with Ytterboe, you know, that black lab that hangs out at St. Olaf. Seems he got to digging in Officer Bill Carroll's garden down on Lincoln Street and his seven-year-old tried to shoo him away by hitting him with a stick. Mrs. Carroll said the dog then nipped her son on the arm, although the skin wasn't broken and she didn't take him to the hospital. But she called the police and said they needed to do something about that dog. So Percy and Tasty Robinson jumped in the squad car and went dog hunting.

"Well, they caught up to him next to the steps that go up to the St. Olaf library. Percy jumped out of the car with the sawed-off shotgun they keep intimidatingly displayed in between the two front seats and blasted away, even though students were laying around on the hill studying or trying to make dates or just bull-shitting. He missed with the first shot but hit the dog with double-aught buckshot the next time, killing him. Then they piled the bloody corpse into the trunk of the squad car and came back to the office to tell of their derring-do."

It didn't take long for the news to travel around the St. Olaf campus. Most of the students liked Ytterboe, fed him snacks, petted him, and regarded him as part of campus life and a reminder of their homes in small towns all over Minnesota. Everybody was outraged by the murder of their mascot and they fired up the east-side Carleton College students to join the cause. By 7:00 pm there were 2500 students and some locals gathered in the street for a block in either direction and up the Third Street hill facing the City Hall.

People were yelling "Give us Percy! Give us Percy!" Others yelled, "Murderers! Murderers!" as Joseph Lee Heywood had done before getting hit on the head with the butt of a pistol.

Lenno Brandt, Chief of Police, placed his five foot six 400 pound frame, breaker of three steering wheels on the squad car in the last year, in front of the City Hall door and yelled back at the crowd, "I'm not giving him to you so get the hell out of here! Go back to your dormitories and stop disturbing the peace!" That only served to heighten the tension and lead to more blasphemous language from the crowd.

"Looks like the crowd is seething with resentment," said Bud. "Do you think they are going to storm the police station?"

"They better not or a lot of people are going to get hurt," said Bob Sletten.

The state patrolman piped up. "We've got the town ringed by state police. If it gets much worse, I give the signal and they all come in to control the crowd. And if that doesn't work, we call in the National Guard."

"Uffda, this could get real ugly," said Bud. "Worse even than when we tried to burn the Carl's bonfire back when I was a student at St. Olaf. A lot of heads and limbs got busted up in that bit of madness. My friend, Matt Kern, was hauling loads of guys up to the infirmary at St. Olaf, some of them riding on the fenders of his old green Studebaker like slain deer."

Pretty soon Mark Almli, Dean of Men at St. Olaf showed up and stood towering over Chief Brandt. Holding his right arm out in front of him with two fingers outstretched, as he often did when chastising freshmen students, he beseeched the crowd to return to their campuses. But the revelers would have none of it and booed him into retreat.

A similar attempt by Merrill Jarchow, Carleton's Dean of Men, resulted in even more invective. "Get out of here, Jarchow, and take your bitch Almli with you!"

Half a dozen highway patrol cars inched slowly through the mob, being careful not to hit anyone, with the wide-eyed inhabitants meeting the glares of hundreds of students. Their attempt to dispirit the restless crowd a failure, and recognizing they were outnumbered, they retreated to the edges of town to await further orders.

And then Fubar arrived. The "gang" that had been falsely suspected of being behind the student robberies took up places on the steps of City Hall. They had been in Lakeville drinking and planning a funeral for Ytterboe when they learned of the mayhem going on in Northfield. The member known as Hoz had been drafting an oration modeled after Marc Antony's speech in *Julius Caesar*. Now he was appealing to the crowd for quiet and to listen to their leader, the one named Argo give the speech.

"Friends, Oles, Countrymen – Lend me your ears! We are come to praise Ytterboe, not to bury him, for the evil that dogs do lives after them, the good is oft interred within their bones. So be the case with Ytterboe, for we so loved our faithful mascot. The noble Percy hath told you that Ytterboe was ambitious. If this were so, it were a grievous fault, and grievously hath Ytterboe answered it, shot in coldest blood on our campus..."

As the crowd assumed their role in the drama, there was a back and forth between them and Argo, as it was in the case in *Julius Caesar*. But then Argo switched to a more reflective stance, asking the crowd to let him "tell you of Ytterboe and his magnificent lineage, where he was born, his humble education, his duties in life." Whereupon they learned that he was born out of wedlock on a dusty street in Dundas in 1949, adopted the name Ytterboe Ole Olaf and moved to Northfield where he found "meaning, truth, and validity on these very streets you stand upon this evening."

The crowd roared with laughter and the mood changed from one of anger to one of humor and frivolity. The crowd asked Argo to tell them more of Ytterboe's life in the "Town of Cows Colleges and Contentment" and Argo obliged, to their great amusement. Finally, he ended the event by leading a funeral dirge "Ytterboe is Dead" to the tune of the Volga Boatman. The dirge went on for several dozen iterations as the crowd slowly dispersed. Another Fubar reminded the crowd that there would be a funeral for Ytterboe on Friday and everyone was invited to attend if they so desired.

Zack had joined Bud and the police officers in front of the cab office. Bud said to Zack, "Well that's your Fubar Gang for you. Quite the violent bunch, huh?"

"Amazing," said Zack. "The trench coat man just made all that shit up!"

The Highway Patrolman observed, "Well, that was the most civilized riot I have ever seen. Guess I'll tell all the boys to go on home. Nothing happening here."

Bob Sletten just shook his head and walked off, confounded by all that just transpired in the course of three or four hours. Fat chuckled and went back into the cab office.

But, of course, it did not end there. All the national broadcast networks, newspapers, and many magazines were informed of the episode and the upcoming funeral. One of the reporters for the *Manitou Messenger* was interviewed on national TV and, for her efforts, was called in by the Vice President of the college and told to keep her mouth shut "or else." Argo, the Fubar whose humorous oration defused the angry mob and prevented it from turning violent, was called in by the Dean of Men, apparently unaware of the events that occurred downtown after he was booed off stage, and read the riot act. Although Argo had no control over the funeral proceedings, he was told not to allow any religious or quasi-religious comments to be made during the funeral "or else" he would be kicked out of the college.

Bud attended the funeral, standing on the hill near the library. Some students had retrieved the body of Ytterboe from the city dump and hid it until it was time for the funeral. The infirmary doctor tested the remains for rabies, an examination not performed by city authorities. Someone obtained an old black hearse for the occasion. The president of Carleton was there to pay his respects. Students read poetry and sang songs in honor of Ytterboe. It was all a very dignified and solemn occasion. And the news media turned their reporters loose on the funeral for a beloved dog taking place on the college campus in the little town where he met his demise. There was TV coverage and a multi-page article with many pictures in *Look Magazine*. Ytterboe was dead.

10 DESIREE'S PREY

Squint hailed Zack as he went by his office on the cement bridge. Zack pulled over at the east end of the bridge and waited for Squint to hobble up to the cab. "Bud told me you two were looking for leads on the college student robberies. I think I may have something for you," said Squint.

"Get in the cab," said Zack. "You have any place you want to go?" asked Zack. "We can talk on the way."

"Take me to Dundas, the Corner Bar," said Squint.

Zack called in his destination and then said to Squint, "OK. What have you got?"

"Well, I been watching things over on the west side. I saw Billy Griffin driving his blue and white Merc up toward St. Olaf Avenue about 9 o'clock one night. He had Clarence from the Flying A in the passenger seat and a couple of other guys in the back. I couldn't make out who they were. But I know Clarence is close friends with Milt Grubbs, the bartender at The Crow's Nest. So I suspect he may have been one of the guys in the back seat. Clarence is a smug ass-hole who likes to brag about his friendship with Milt. Anyway, so I just kinda put that in the back of my head and kept my good eye on the goings-on at the bar. Sometimes Milt would go off with Clarence for a cigarette. Now, mind you, they didn't do anything improper that I saw but..."

Zack finished Squint's sentence, "But it made you kind of suspicious, didn't it?"

"Yeah. So I got Lonnie van Guilder and we went into the bar and had a couple of beers. I tried to eavesdrop on Milt's conversations with customers but couldn't make out very much. You know that Desiree Goodlove hangs out in there?"

"No, but it doesn't surprise me."

"Well, she and Milt have got some kind of thing going there. He'll fetch her over to meet some guy he's talking to and before long they'll be leaving together."

"Think he's pimping her out?" asked Zack.

"Could be," observed Squint.

As they turned off Highway 3 into Dundas, Squint said, "I was down here a couple of days ago and overheard some guy talking about something big going down in Northfield before long. Didn't know who he was. He was pretty drunk and pissing and moaning about some guy walking off with his girlfriend."

As Squint got out of the car, Zack thanked him for the information and encouraged him to keep watching. H'm, he thought to himself, maybe we have some new suspects.

"Five vacant in Dundas," Zack spoke into the microphone.

"Pick up Mrs. Cruz and bring her back to town," Fat's voice came back on the speaker.

Zack knew that meant picking up the stout little middle-aged lady with a mustache along with a passel of her kids. They were not her biological children but severely impaired foster children she cared for. No one else wanted to take on that kind of burden yet she seemed to take their foibles in stride and with good humor.

As Mrs. Cruz and an older girl struggled to contain the thrashing arms and legs of two of the young children, Zack said, "Good day, Mrs. Cruz. Where would you like to go today?"

"Take us to Doc Lufkin's office. Got a sick little one here that needs some medication."

***

The demoralization in the police department after the Ytterboe debacle was not wasted on Milt Grubbs. There had been virtually no reports of the college student robberies in the local newspapers and Milt wondered what Lenno Brandt might be up to. Were they just that incompetent or were they laying some kind of trap for his gang? Reports had reached him of people asking about his finances and his associates. It seemed like a good time to call in his version of Mata Hari, Desiree Goodlove.

"Des, you know anyone in the police department?" asked Milt.

"I know a couple of the officers, or rather, they know me," said Des with a smirk. "And I kinda know their new dispatcher, Derwood Attwater. He's kind of a dork but not a real stuffed shirt or pain in the ass like the others. I see him down at the Muni now and then."

"Do you suppose you could strike up a friendship next time you run into him, find out if Lenno is investigating anything of importance lately?"

"I'll see what I can do," said Des. "There may be some expenses. You up for that?"

"Within reason," said Milt. "Get back to me when you have something."

Des liked the idea of working "undercover" even if it was for the wrong side because she could fantasize herself playing a role in a drama where she would obtain acclaim as a movie star. Her sole skill for which she felt self-confidence was as a seductress. She never displayed any talent while in high school, never achieved any academic excellence, never participated in any sports. But when it came to getting men to salivate over tempting pleasures of the flesh, she was the siren of Northfield, the coquette of Rice County, the vamp of the North Star state.

Like any skilled craftsperson or expert performer, she was self-consciously aware of what she was doing every step of the way, from the furtive eye contact to the flattery, from the simulated interest in his every word to the sexually suggestive commentary, from the fake demureness to playing footsies under the table, from the gentle touching of his hand to the assertive resting of her hand on his thigh. She wore the right kind of clothes for her dalliance: a blouse that revealed just enough breast to draw attention with nipples evident under the thin fabric, frayed short-shorts that allowed her pubic region to be easily accessed by groping fingers of the gentleman's hand she placed there, attire that could be quickly shed for an impetuous fling in the back seat of a car.

Des's prey, Derwood Attwater, was a timid, self-effacing young man who had moved to Northfield from Farmington when he got the job of police dispatcher. That job involved answering the telephone and taking down complaints from citizens reporting a crime or, more likely, being perturbed by some neighbor or the neighbor's barking dog. If a police officer was in the office at the time, he would report it to him and a decision made as to its disposition. If he was alone, he would report the call by two-way radio to whichever officer was in the squad car, driving around. His unassuming manner ensured that he would not create additional woes for the department by antagonizing the citizens, except maybe those who wanted to do something "Right Now!" To those kinds of callers, he would explain that he just answered the phone and did not have any authority to take any action on his own, that he would get the caller's complaint to a police officer as soon as possible.

That usually would let him off the hook for a consumer's outrage.

Des spotted her quarry when he came into the Municipal Liquor Store or "Muni" after work and sat at the bar. He ordered a beer. She got up from her position in a booth and stood next to him as she ordered a Sazerac.

"What's in that?" Derwood inquired with a puzzled look on his face.

"It's made with licorice-flavored liquor, whiskey, bitters, sugar, and a twist of lemon," said Des. It's really good. Wanna taste?"

"No, I'm not much for those fancy drinks," said Derwood.

"Aw, come on, give it a try," said Des, batting her eyelids.

After resisting one more time, Derwood gave in and tried a sip of the drink. "H'm. That is interesting. Has kind of a faint licorice after-taste."

"I knew you'd like it," said Des. "You're new around here aren't you?" she inquired.

"I moved down from Farmington. Been here a few weeks now."

"Yeah. I saw you in here once before. I wanted to introduce myself but I didn't want to be too forward. Are you getting used to the town? Know anyone yet?"

"Oh, gee. I ...I...I've met a few people. I'm kind of shy, so I don't meet a lot of people, ya know?"

"Why don't we go over and sit in a booth. I'd like to get to know you better," said Des coyly as she reached for Derwood's hand and led him to a dark booth in a corner of the bar.

Derwood noted the impression her nipples made in her shirt as she turned around and couldn't keep his eyes off the gyrating gluteus maximus in cut-off Levis sans a belt that led him across the room.

"Let me see your hand," said Des as she reached across the table. "Have you ever had your palm read?"

"No. I don't believe in that stuff," said Derwood.

Des held the back of his hand in her left and stroked his palm with the fingertips of her right hand. Derwood could feel his passion rising but tried to act nonchalant. Des knew what was happening in Derwood's Jockey shorts, of course, but went on talking about his heart line and his lifeline and how he was in for a pleasant surprise shortly. She shed one of her sandals and rubbed her foot on his leg.

"You got a car?" she asked. "I'd like to go for a ride."

By this time Derwood had a full-blown erection and had to adjust his pants to accommodate the protuberance. Des just smiled and rose from her seat, watching his eyes as she smoothed the denim covering her pubis. Once they got in the car, she reached around Derwood's neck and drew him to her for a kiss. Then she took his left hand and placed it on her thigh, pushing his wrist forward until his fingers met the wetness of her vagina. She stroked the rigid member behind Derwood's fly and he started to unbutton her shorts to get a better grasp on the situation. But Des drew his hand away, saying, "Let's wait until we get to my place."

Des directed Derwood to her apartment at the rear of a house on South Linden Street and the two of them made a bee-line for the door. Once inside, they embraced and hurriedly began to shed clothes. Des led the way to her bedroom where a dim floor lamp provided a golden glow to their forms. They explored each other's body first with their fingers and then with their mouths, a bit of Freudian oral incorporation, perhaps, or a kind of primal capture of the spirit of the other. Or maybe it just felt good.

Each quickly attained orgasm but it was less than five minutes later that Derwood entered Des and they achieved another climax. Then Des was on top of Derwood, coaxing his detumescent penis into yet another erection with a combination of manual and oral manipulations. Straddling his hips, she settled her labia around his rigid member and yelled, "Hi-Yo Silver" as she enacted the movements of a rider on horseback, until Derwood and she both groaned with pleasure. While still embedded in her flesh, he rolled her over without loss of rigidity and continued the pleasuring until exhaustion required a break.

Des rolled over on her stomach and after Derwood had recovered, he entered her from behind, her hands reaching down between her legs and encasing his scrotum, giving it a gentle squeeze, a value-added delectation. And so it went, until the wee hours of the morning when both were totally spent.

During cigarette breaks and pillow talk, Des inquired about Derwood's job and if anything interesting was going on in the department. Derwood was only too willing to share what he knew with this angel of carnal delight. He told her of the college student robberies and how they were trying to get information from several sources, including cab drivers Zack and Bud. And he told her that the Fubar had been eliminated as possible suspects but that Milt and Clarence were now being watched as suspicious characters.

**

Late the next day, Des reported to Milt. "Boy, those quiet ones really can give you a workout. Took me a couple of hours after I got out of bed before I could walk straight," she laughed.

Milt grinned. "Did you find out anything?"

"Yeah, you and Clarence are considered suspicious characters. They've been having two of the cab drivers at 777 asking about you. Squint Howard may be another informant, but I'm not sure about that."

"Anything else? They got any plans?"

"Not that Derwood knew of. Just waiting and watching."

"Good work, Des. That's my girl!"

On a break, Milt walked over to see Clarence at the Flying A. He didn't want to reveal the new development to the rest of the gang because he correctly sensed that they might be opposed to the actions he had in mind.

"Let's go over on the bridge and have a cigarette," said Milt.

Squint was in his office as they approached but did not move.

"Hey, Squint. How's it going? Said Milt"

"Tough times a-coming, tough times a-coming," Squint blurted out his usual off-putting message.

"Yeah, they may be coming for you, Squint, if you keep blabbing about my friends to the wrong people. You ever think what it would feel like to go head first over this here railing and down into the river below? Eh, ever think about that? 'Cause, you know, it would probably smart a good deal when you hit the water. Why you might just split your head open on those rocks down there."

Squint thought for a second about giving him the old "eagle claw" grasp of the windpipe and throwing him over the bridge as he had done back in Germany many years ago but quickly discarded the idea as likely having a bad outcome for him. Still, he kept it in mind just in case his opponent made a move toward him.

"Tough times a-coming, tough times a-coming," Squint said again before walking over to the riverside park, muttering under his breath,

"Mudafker, mudafker!"

Milt turned his attention to Clarence. "Clarence, ol buddy, we got a problem. I just learned that those two young drivers for 777 have been asking questions and trying to get information about our little night-time forays. I wonder what we should do about that?"

"Maybe they need to meet with a little accident," offered Clarence.

"It would have to be something that couldn't be tied to us. We'd have to be someplace else when it happened."

"Yeah, let me think about that for a while," said Clarence.

***

Zack had finished his workday and walked up the Third Street hill to retrieve his motorcycle. On Sundays when traffic and business were slow, Zack and Bud would park their motorcycles in the first parking space behind the spots reserved for taxis so they could wash, wax, and otherwise spruce them up between calls. The rest of the week they would park them on Washington Street, behind the library where they were not within their purview.

Zack mounted his Zundapp, pushed the streamlined little key into the receptacle on the headlight, and gave a downward kick on the starter crank, bringing the opposed-twin to life immediately. He let it idle a bit before pulling in the clutch lever and using his left toe to lift the gear lever into first. Letting the clutch out, he moved slowly from the parking spot down Washington to Fourth Street where he made a gliding "Northfield stop" and rounded the corner to go down the hill.

About two-thirds of the way down the hill, he applied the brakes to stop at Bridge Square. But nothing happened, he didn't slow down. Panicking as he approached the intersection and fearful that he would get hit broadside by a vehicle, his options came in a flash. Either lay the motorcycle down on its side and slide to a stop, hoping his street-side leg didn't get too mangled and no cars ran him over on the way. Or chance it, stay upright and aim for the little spot of grass next to the popcorn stand on the island across from the post office. Then lay it down, digging the handlebar into the dirt for a somewhat controlled crash.

Opting for the latter, he zoomed across Division Street. Horns blared as he narrowly avoided getting hit by a car, hit the curb surrounding the island, bounced up, glazed the monument to war veterans in the center of the island, but managed to swing his weight and get the machine to slide to a stop on the left cylinder head and left footrest. Amazingly, his leg was in the space between the ground and the gas tank, so he received no broken bones. Only a scratched-up and bruised hip, left arm and left temple.

Holy shit, he thought as he lay on his side. That could have been the end of Zack Buckler! People came running to lift the motorcycle and help Zack to stand, quickly transferring him to the base of the marble monument.

"What happened?" everyone asked. Spurred out of his daze by the question, Zack looked at his mangled motorcycle then asked a couple of men to help him get over to take a look at the front wheel and brake mechanism on the back wheel. He reached down and pulled the unattached brake cable from the front wheel. Then he operated the back brake pedal which was on the right side of the bike. It moved to the bottom of the stroke with no resistance. Not likely that both mechanisms would go out at the same time, he thought. They had to have been purposely disabled. "Someone's trying to kill me," he said out loud.

Zack was off work for a couple of days. The police had confiscated his Zundapp to hold until forensic experts from the county could come and dust for fingerprints. When he came back into the office, everyone peppered him with questions. Was it the jealous boyfriend of someone he had bedded? Did someone have a grudge against him? What had he been up to that would make someone want to sabotage his motorcycle?

Zack had asked all those questions of himself but couldn't come up with any real suspects. It had to be someone with mechanical knowledge about motorcycles but that could be just about any male in town. And anyone with a brain would have worn gloves, so the fingerprint check would be unlikely to come up with anything. Could it be that they were ticking off the people behind these robberies? Maybe, but where is the evidence? You can't just go around accusing people of a crime without any evidence. Bud agreed but said he was getting worried about their safety. What might they try next?

Bud didn't have to wait long to find out. He had drawn the 1953 Plymouth to drive, the most over-ripe lemon of the fleet of lemons that made up the Northfield Cab Company. It had just been over at the Flying A to get an oil change and change its toilet paper oil filter, a contraption on all the cars that reduced the cost of upkeep considerably by using a roll of toilet paper instead of an expensive commercial oil filter. He had made several calls already when columnist Maggie Lee walked into the cab stand from her office at the *Northfield News,* half a dozen doors south of the cab stand.

11 CAR TROUBLE

"Where to, Maggie?" asked Bud. Maggie was a tall, lanky woman who started as a bookkeeper but quickly transformed into a reporter and editor of one of the two local newspapers. Not a ravishing beauty nor given to the latest fashion, she was pleasant enough looking and was usually cheerful and talkative.

"Take me to Carleton, Laird Hall. I'm going to interview Larry Gould. Did you know he is only the fourth president of the college.?"

"Yes, I used to deliver his Minneapolis newspaper every morning when I had a paper route covering that part of town," said Bud. "He was friendly, used to have me come into his office and he'd say a few words, asked what I liked to do, that sort of thing. I never had much to say. I knew he was a big arctic explorer, though."

"He became president of Carleton in 1945, a year after I started with the *News*. I'm going to interview him about his plans for the college. He's added a lot of faculty and brought in big bucks for the endowment fund."

Bud had shifted into second gear and was just

about to turn the corner to go up the steep Second Street hill when there was a jolt and a loud bang, followed by an eerie screeching sound. Looking out his door window and seeing sparks flying by, he realized that his seat was just a few inches off the ground. He quickly concluded that he had lost his left front wheel and was headed toward the one-story cinder block building where newsboys would pick up their bundle of papers for the day.

"Hold on to the dash," Bud yelled to Maggie as the brake drum dug into the pavement, twirling them around like a bumper car in an amusement park. He was still trying to turn the steering wheel but it had a mind of its own. The brake line must have broken since the brake pedal went completely to the floor without any resistance. He pulled on the emergency brake which supplied some drag to the rear wheels. Finally, they jumped the curb and came to rest in the side yard of the Truax house. Maggie had bumped her head but wasn't bleeding. Bud had a sore chest where he had slammed into the steering wheel and a sore left knee where he collided with the bottom of the dashboard.

"Oh my god, we could have been killed," shrieked Maggie before she broke into uncontrollable laughter and said, wryly, "I guess I'll have to reschedule that interview! But I got first-hand experience for a new column, so that is the positive takeaway."

Bud joined in the relief laughter. "Oh shit! Guess I won't get a tip on this fare will I!"

The Fire Department arrived in minutes and extracted the pair from the disabled vehicle. Satisfied there were no injuries requiring transport to the hospital, the firemen returned the emergency vehicle to its usual haunt, giving Maggie a ride back to the office of the *Northfield News* in the process.

Bob Sletten and Tasty Robinson pulled up in the squad car. Tasty directed traffic away from the accident scene and Bob moved in to examine the vehicle.

"Looks like your lug nuts came loose on that wheel," he said. "When was the last time you had it worked on?"

"Had an oil change last night at the Flying A but I used it all morning without any trouble.

"Yeah, they can work themselves loose gradually. But usually, it only takes a couple of them to hold the wheel on. Have you had any flat tires lately?"

"No. The last time we had any wheel work done was when we changed from snow tires to regular tires last April."

"I'll go over to Flying A and see if they did anything with your wheels during your oil change. I doubt it but I'll check it out. In the meantime, I'll have the wrecker come to haul this car off to the junkyard down next to the Fifth Street Bridge. You don't think Fat wants to keep it do you?"

"Here he comes now. Why don't you ask him?"

Zack drove up in his cab with Fat in the passenger seat. "Holy shit!" exclaimed Zack. "What happened?

"Wheel fell off," said Bud. "Seems like the lug nuts worked themselves loose."

"Yeah, like my brake lines came loose! Somebody is trying to do us grave bodily harm," said Zack.

"You OK?" asked Fat. "How's Maggie?"

"We were both lucky as hell. We got a little bunged-up but nothing serious. Sure could have been, though. I think Zack has something there – somebody doesn't seem to like us nosing around about the robberies."

"I think maybe you two should come over and talk to me and Lenno about where you have been and what you've learned," said Sletten. This certainly sounds like a suspicious situation."

***

Sletten went over to Flying A to find out who had worked on Bud's car. Clarence was off that night so one of the other attendants did the oil change. No, the wheels were not removed or even touched during the process but the air pressure in the tires was checked. The car had been stored overnight in the alley alongside the station after it had been worked on. No, no one was seen walking around the alley, but it was dark and the night-time attendant was busy tending to customers or watching a ball game on TV.

Fat had the lug nuts on all the other cabs checked to make sure there weren't other accidents about to happen. Zack and Bud met with Lenno & Sletten to go over where they had been, who they had talked with, any reactions they had observed from anyone. No hard evidence could be turned up that implicated any particular suspect.

But then Squint hailed Zach on one of his trips over the cement bridge. He got into the cab and they drove around the block. He told Zach about his encounter with Clarence and Milt a few days earlier, about how Milt had threatened to throw him over the bridge if he didn't keep his mouth shut about his friends.

"What did you say?" asked Zach.

"I just gave him one of my unintelligible muttering responses," said Squit, sounding uncharacteristically alert and intelligible.

"Do you know what friends he was referring to?" asked Zach.

"Well, Clarence was right there with him. He was one of them and I know Dale Halverson hangs out with them."

"Dale Halverson? You mean Becky's brother?"

"The guy that drives for Pop Jones at 1100. I don't know if he has a sister. Might be."

Zack thought of the conversation he had with Becky about how her brother's unsavory association with Milt and Clarence made her and her parents mad. H'm. Is Squint on to something here?

"Are you willing to keep watching these guys or did they scare you off?" asked Zach.

"They made me mad as hell but I kept my

cool and walked away, just acted like I was crazy and scared. I'd like to throw those bastards off the bridge but I know we need to get the goods on them if we want to send them to the Graybar Hotel."

"Don't get too close so you antagonize them. We don't want you to have any accidents like Bud and I had recently."

"I heard about that. I can still handle myself in a one-to-one fight but might not fare too well if they all gang up on me, so I'll be careful. I'll let you know if I get something solid to go on."

***

While officer Sletten was over at Flying A checking out the work on Bud's cab, he decided to go into the Owl's Nest to nose around. Sletten had been trained by Barney Wells, the police chief before Lenno Brandt took over. Wells was a Native American who preferred to walk a beat in downtown Northfield rather than ride around in a squad car. Those who lived there at the time would see Barney leaning up against a light pole over on the west side, apparently picking his teeth from a snack he had at brother Friggie's cafe. At other times he would be enjoying the afternoon shade as he leaned against the wall of Bierman's Furniture Store or he might show up standing in front of the *Northfield News*. In truth his style was a lesson in "studied nonchalance" as he was actually observing everything that was going on around him, noting patterns and deviation from patterns of behavior and giving off no indication of what he was doing. Barney was the kind of police officer who could influence adolescent behavior by a mere glance and discourage reckless driving by a scowl. Unfortunately, he lost his position when he failed to arrest the son of a prominent merchant whose drunk driving of a fire truck after a celebration resulted in a tragic crash and loss of life on the St. Olaf campus. Long-time residents were disappointed to see Barney go but recognized he had made a serious error in judgment.

Sletten liked Barney's indirect approach to data gathering and finding the truth. He thought he might be able to rattle some cages and see if anyone reacted unusually when he went into the Crow's Nest. The eyes of all patrons were glued on him as he entered the bar, a first for all of them.

"Hello, Mr. Grubbs. I was in the area checking on some unusual accidents and thought I would see if you or any of your customers saw anything unusual three nights ago. Did you see anyone walking around the alley next to the Flying A after 11:00 on Tuesday?"

Mr. Grubbs? Nobody calls me that, Milt thought unless they already have checked up on me. I have never talked with this officer. What is he up to?

"Why, no, officer. I'm always behind the bar so I wouldn't see anything going on out there unless I carried some trash out to the garbage bin. And I don't remember anything unusual in the last few

nights. We always get a few customers that im-
bibe too much and go out there to puke. But that's
typical around here. Did something happen in this
alley that's connected to the accidents you are asking about?"

"I can't really say at this point," said Sletten,
being deliberately and obviously evasive. Thinking
he would push Milt a little further by suggesting
he might be a suspect, he asked, "How long have
you worked at this bar now, Mr. Grubbs?"

"I've been here about 2 years now," said Milt. "Is
that important?"

"No, no, just curious," said Sletten as he strode
over to where Desiree Goodlove was sitting.

"Hi, Des. You're out pretty early today. You keeping busy?"

"Certainly, Officer Sletten," said Des as she
flashed a crossed arms coquettish pose. "You know
what they say, 'The early bird gets worms,' don't
you?"

Looking around at the other patrons, Sletten
broadened his inquiry beyond the alley and three
days ago, primarily for the benefit of Milt. "Anyone
else seen anything unusual over here lately?"

No one responded. "Well, if you remember anything you know where to find me. Or you can just
call with any tip you have to share with the police.
Thanks for being good citizens."

After Sletten left, Des came over to Milt at the
bar. "What do you think he is up to?" she asked.

"I don't know," said Milt. "He's probably just trying to shake something out of the woodwork, see if he can get someone to talk. If he had anything to make charges on, he'd have taken some action, pulled someone into the police station for a talk. But he does have some suspicions about me or this place, so that is a concern. Maybe I'll have to have another talk with Clarence."

***

Once the sheriff was finished examining his smashed-up Zundapp, Zack rented a trailer at Finney's and hauled the bike up to Franklin Avenue in Minneapolis where it could be repaired. The engine and frame had survived the crash with just scratches but the front fork had to be replaced and both fenders pounded out and repainted. The mechanics at the German Motorcycle Company all knew Zack and assured him they would get it back in like-new condition.

In the meantime, Zack continued his courtship of Becky in his Plymouth coupe, but not as enthusiastically as before. He couldn't put his finger on it but there was something about their relationship that gave him pause, some intuition that theirs might not be a good fit. He made excuses why he couldn't see her on more than one occasion and his resistance to the sirens at the Viking Cafe was wearing down.

For her part, Becky knew from the decrease in the frequency of their dates and the lame excuses he proffered that Zack was having second thoughts about their relationship and suspected he might be being unfaithful. Although she had no concrete evidence to go on, she felt betrayed and insecure. She asked herself what she might have done to alienate the one she loved. Had she not adequately verbalized her loyalty and commitment? Did she not provide the practical support and security she thought he must need, especially since he had lost his parents so early in life? Did she not support and encourage his pursuits? Was she not physically attractive enough?

Becky couldn't provide a convincing affirmative answer to any of these inquiries. Maybe, she thought, she harbored an unconscious wish to end the relationship and find a less introspective and more practical mate, one who complimented her inclinations. But this line of psychologizing, turning herself into the betrayer, only added a dose of guilt to her worrying.

Finally, she came to the tentative conclusion that she was being unappreciated, taken for granted, used. She became even more negative, found it hard to tolerate the unfamiliar, and was even more fanciful about a looming catastrophe. Without being able to access the empirical evidence and reasonable thought processes she typically relied upon to make decisions, she could feel the disappointment, anger, and bitterness bubbling up in her chest.

So, when another would-be suitor, Charley Weldon, made his 20th attempt to date her, Becky impulsively agreed. She'd show Zack that she didn't need him, that other men found her attractive. It was a move made out of spite and one she would later regret. But she had abandoned her usual self and wanted to be adventurous and try this "spontaneity thing" rather than being her loyal, responsible and traditional self. Whenever anything new to her was suggested, she now asked herself, "Why not?" and went along with the suggestion. Why not go dancing 'til the wee hours? Why not get drunk? Why not let Charley stick his fingers in her vagina? Why not shuck his corn? What the hell, who cares anyway?

When Zack did finally pay a visit, Becky expressed her concern about his life being threatened when he crashed his motorcycle on Bridge Square. Her parents were not so sure it wasn't just an accident because of "those unsafe motorcycles." They couldn't believe that anyone in Northfield would deliberately try to kill a nice young man like Zack.

Becky continued to voice her concern about her brother and now, after the crash, Zack also had an interest in Dale's activities. Was he involved in the attempt on Zack's life? Zack didn't know but he found it curious that Dale didn't mention the incident when Zack first came up to the house afterward. Wouldn't he have had at least a little curiosity about an event that nearly claimed his sister's boyfriend's life? Once it was being openly discussed, Dale made some innocuous inquiries about what it felt like to go barreling across Bridge Square but Dale's commiseration just didn't feel genuine to Zack.

So Zack began to ask Dale about his plans for the future, posing various educational options he could pursue, but Dale had reasons that none of them would work for him. Zack asked about Dale's friends and Dale continued to deflect the inquiry. Becky became uncomfortable because Zack's questioning began to sound more like a grilling than helpful inquiry, so she suggested that she and Zack go for a ride. Zack felt he might have pushed a little too hard without having any real evidence that Dale was involved in his motorcycle crash and so backed off. But he was even more suspicious than before.

Becky and Zack drove the 15 miles down to Faribault and stopped at a drive-in for cheeseburgers, fries and vanilla shakes. Becky again brought up her concerns about her brother.

"He's gone all the time, hanging out with a bunch of losers. They went up to the River Road Club under the Mendota Bridge on Friday and saw Chubby Checkers and then went over to Doc Evans's place and listened to jazz and drank setups until the place closed. Came home in the middle of the night, half lit up. Next thing you know he'll be going up to the Key Club and that South of the Border place, taking up with those streetwalkers that hang out there, coming home with some dreaded disease. Yuk!

"Then yesterday he comes home with a new pistol, says he's going to become an expert shot, enter competitions and win prizes. I don't know where he got that idea or where he got the money to buy the gun. He said he's gotten a lot of tips recently from fares he has driving cab. Mom said she didn't want the gun in the house but dad thought it was a good idea for him to learn how to shoot just in case he needs to use it sometime. Dad always likes to be prepared for any untoward events."

"They must have better-heeled fares over at 1100 then we get at 777," said Zack with a hint of sarcasm. "Now let me get this right, Dale is friends with Milt Grubbs, Clarence Dixon, and Billy Griffin, right?"

"Right. They've been friends since high school. Then there is Howard Kinlaw. He just joined their group. He used to be a Carleton student."

"Kinlaw, h'm," pause. "From what I've been able to glean talking with him, Dale doesn't sound like he wants to learn anything, develop a skill or advance himself in any way. And he's hanging out with these bozos doing what? Do you know where they go, what they do?"

"Not really. I guess they just hang out together, drink beer, go nightclubbing, play pool, go to ball games. I don't know. When I ask him why he hangs out with them, he just says that it's exciting."

"Exciting? Yeah, maybe real exciting! Like pulling stick-ups and causing accidents that could kill someone, yours truly included!"

"No! You don't think Dale could do that, do you? He's my little brother. I know he's been in some scrapes with the law before but they were just pranks, nothing serious like you are suggesting."

"Maybe not, but Becky, I think Dale might be involved with the gang that is robbing college students. If he is mixed up in that he could be charged with a felony or even attempted murder if he had anything to do with the accidents that Bud and I both had."

"Oh my god. I don't know what to do," said Becky as she became viably more distraught. "I don't want to go home. I need a hug. I need to be held. I have to get my mind off of this. Can we go somewhere where we can be alone?"

Zack drove to the $6 Motel and rented a room. They turned on the TV and lay in bed with the pillows pushed up against the wall. Becky snuggled up under Zack's left arm and told him she felt safe and secure in his arms. She slide her left hand back and forth on his chest and gradually ventured south to find Zack's little soldier standing at attention. He kissed her and fondled her breasts over her blouse as she unzipped his pants. Both stood up and shed their clothes, Becky neatly folding hers and laying them on a chair while Zack threw his off in a heap on the floor. Climbing back into bed, pillows now in their normal position, they continued to touch each other in all the forbidden places.

Taking Zack's right hand in hers, she pressed his

middle finger into her vagina, up against her clitoris, and began moving it in and out, up and down. If he was so bold as to innovate in his motions, she would again grab his finger and demonstrate the way she wanted him to do it.

"No, no. This is the way I want you to do it. This is the way it feels best. Keep doing it like this."

Zack complied with her wishes, getting more aroused as he saw she was approaching climax. He smiled when she began breathing heavily, let out a snort, and finally a gasp. As he moved to enter her, she again restrained him.

"Let me do this," she said. Pushing him flat on his back, she sat up along his side and put two of his fingers in her vagina. Grasping his penis with her right hand and his scrotum with her left, she began simultaneously massaging his testicles while she moved her penis hand up and down, slowly for quite some time as his tension mounted and then more rapidly as he neared ejaculation. When the inevitable eruption occurred, it was with such force as to shoot several feet into the air, coming to rest on her hand and Zack's chest. She kept moving her penis hand at a slow rate until all excretions were in abeyance, rubbing the moistened tip with her fingers. Zack rose to kiss her and then dropped back on the bed to recover.

"Did you like that?" asked Becky. "I love to touch you like that. I've always wondered what it is like to have a penis and now I feel like I almost have one."

"Yes, yes it was good," said Zack. "You have a wonderful touch," he said, trying to be complimentary.

But he was not satisfied and soon his erection was on the way back. Becky played with it some more and massaged his testicles until it was again in a rigid state. Then she climbed aboard Zack, rising above his mauve member and guiding it into her enveloping vagina.

Both of them watched the conjunction of their body parts as they appeared and disappeared from view when she made her pelvic thrusts. The visual input heightened their passions. Zack felt enclosed and stimulated from all sides as Becky continued her rhythmic movements and Becky was able to move her clitoris into the proper position for maximal pleasure with her on the top side. Zack got into the rhythm of Becky's movements and lifted his hips to maximize penetration on the downstroke. Zack tried to hold back until he saw that Becky was about to come before he unleashed his colossal orgasm. Becky collapsed on Zack's chest with her breasts immersed in the remains of his initial ejaculate. She left his penis in her, focusing on the sensations and occasionally giving a vaginal squeeze until it retreated of its own accord.

After their musculature recovered enough for normal upright movement, they got into the bathtub and washed each other while also touching, rubbing, and kissing each other. Zack began to get another erection and wanted to try out some other tricks but Becky vetoed it, saying she had to get home or her parents would be worried.

On the way back to Northfield, Becky again mentioned her concern about her brother and her belief that he couldn't be involved in the mishaps that befell Zack and Bud.

"You won't do anything to implicate him without any evidence would you, Zack?"

"No, Becky. I'd have to have more to go on than I have now. But I don't like the fact that he is hanging out with a crowd that is suspected of strong-arming college kids."

"Can you let me try to convince him to mend his ways before you go any further with this?"

"I'm not trying to railroad your brother into anything, Becky. You go ahead and talk to him, let him know he is under suspicion. Maybe he'll shape up, maybe not."

Zack was mostly silent for the remainder of their journey, reflecting on what had happened and wondering about Becky's motivation. The sex was pleasurable. Well, more pleasurable than not having any. But what's with all this controlling and directing the way it is to go? Is she a control freak? Does she always have to be in charge? Does she always have to be on top? Can't I introduce any of my variations? Zack reflected on his earlier relationship with the woman who had broken his heart a couple of years ago. They were so attuned to each other that they could anticipate each other's moves and enhance them. They knew and accepted what each other wanted and mostly achieved climax at the same time. Sex with that woman was intuitive and easy. It felt like a merging of souls.

Or was this whole day just a set-up to get me to lay off her brother? That would be a game-changer since Zack had zero tolerance for being manipulated.

He was on the verge of confronting Becky about his doubts and uneasiness with her but kept himself in check. Just calm down, let it go, for now, he told himself. Don't come out with a bunch of accusations. Make sure you are clear about the facts and your motives.

12 CELEBRATING AN OUTLAW

"Gimme a carton of Luckies," said Bud as he walked up to the counter in Tiny's Smoke Shop.

"That'll be $2.50," said Tiny all decked out in beard and cowboy hat. His patrons were all looking quite grizzled too, sporting beards, boots, and cowboy garb. Aphorisms borrowed from western programs on TV were freely sprinkled in their speech: "Howdy, pardner!" "Guess I'll giddy-up home." "Reckon that'll suit me just fine."

Signs of the impending Defeat of Jesse James Days Fall Festival were everywhere. Merchants had displays of "old stuff" in their shop windows and Civil War-era bunting adorned most downtown buildings. The motels on the north end of town were filling up as was the Stuart Hotel (which opened in 1877 as the Archer House the year after the famous bank raid). Workers erected a large sign reading "BANK" above the old 112 cab office next to the Quality Bakery. A carnival was being assembled behind the Malt O'Meal plant (the old Ames Mill) where the ice skating rink sits during the winter months.

Johnny Western, a country singer-songwriter, musician, actor, and radio host who grew up in Northfield, returned from Hollywood after striking it big with his song *The Ballad of Paladin* aired weekly on the TV show *Have Gun - Will Travel.* The local boy-who-made-good managed to persuade his friend, Johnny Cash, and a couple of other musicians to accompany him in playing for the crowds off a flatbed truck situated on Water Street next to the US. Post Office building.

Signs were everywhere announcing the times and places for various events – the soapbox derby on West Third Street, near St. John's Lutheran Church; the parade on Sunday starting at the Northfield Cemetery on South Division Street; a car to be given away could be seen over near the carnival grounds; a golf tournament to be held at the course at Prairie and Seventh Street; Bingo on Bridge Square; the bank raid re-enactments on Friday, Saturday and Sunday; and a popcorn maker in a simulated old rail car was rolled into the area where Zack had smashed his motorcycle. In the same area, saw-horse like barricades were moved onto the corners where streets were to be blocked off. Rumors circulated about "unofficial" drag races taking place in locations to be announced shortly before they occurred.

Bud stopped into Laura Baddgor's place for a cup of coffee on his way back to the cab office. It was apparent she had just been engaged in a contentious interchange with a local businessman about the forthcoming celebrations.

"It's all a commercialization propagated by the Jaycees of an old event that celebrates an outlaw," screamed Laura.

She poured Bud's coffee into a mug that had seen so many refills its porcelain had developed pits around the rim. Setting it down on the counter, she sought allies to support her views. "What do you young whippersnappers think of all this folderol, Bud?"

Bud liked Laura and he knew she liked him because she always treated him with respect and went out of her way to give him something extra on his orders. But he knew he was being set up and didn't want to get into the middle of one of her spats with the local cognoscenti.

"Well, I can't speak for all young whippersnappers, just myself. I know that most merchants appreciate it and benefit from it and the townsfolk enjoy all the festivities before the long cold winter sets in, even if it does mess up traffic flow for a time. But I also know there are those like my former social studies teacher who take a dim view of throwing a party for an outlaw. And before you bring it up, I know they have added the 'Defeat of' prefix to the name. But everyone knows it is the Jesse James name that draws the crowds. So I guess, I would have to say it is a mixed blessing."

Laura smiled at Bud's recognition of her ploy and his diplomatic avoidance of raising the ire of any of the cafe's onlookers. That boy's going to go places, she thought. "Well played," she said out loud as Bud picked up his cup and departed. He could hear the din of debaters resume as he walked past Grant Electric and into the cab office.

All the cabbies were growing mustaches and beards. Even Fat sprouted a small brush under his nose. Of course, they all poked fun at each other's efforts and conceded no contest to Tiny's whopping face fungus.

The 777 phone rang and Fat answered. After listening to the voice on the other end for longer than usual, he said "That will cost you about $50." Pause. "Yes mam, right away."

Addressing Bud, he said "There's a reporter over at the Stuart Hotel who wants to get a first-hand view of the important places for DJJD. She has a camera and will want to stop and take pictures. I told her the total fare would be $50, assuming it takes about five hours."

"Gotcha, boss," said Bud as he went out the door. Going down Division to Second Street, Bud made a U-turn and parked in front of the hotel. An attractive woman that he estimated to be in her thirties, carrying a camera bag and purse, came down the steps and got in the back seat.

"Hi, I'm Lucy Palan," she said sticking out her hand. "What should I call you?"

"Just call me Bud. Where would you like to go first?"

"Well, why don't you give me an overview of

the bank robbery and how the gang escaped, where they were captured."

"Yes, mam," said Bud. "Well, the gang was around here for a couple of days before they tried to rob the bank. On the day of the raid, they had a meal at Jeft's Diner, made a final inspection of the town, and then assembled up on West Third Street west of where the Odd Fellows Home is now. Do you want to go there?"

"Sure," said his passenger. "I want to get a feel for the whole operation before I see the re-enactment."

They proceeded to West Third Street and the reporter took pictures of the railroad depot and the grove of trees where the gang made their vote to rob the bank. Then they traveled to the site of the bank, next to the Scriver Building on Bridge Square where Anselm R. Manning shot Bill Stiles from his horse 75 yards down the block and wounded Cole Younger. The passenger took several photos of the old cab stand with the wooden "BANK" sign above it as well as the Scriver Building, Bridge Square, and the building across the street from which Henry Wheeler shot Clell Miller dead and wounded Bob Younger. They moved up Division Street to the Fifth Street intersection where Cole Younger shot Swedish immigrant, Nicholas Gustafson.

Acting as a tour guide, Bud related the essence of the story: "After the gang gave up their effort to rob the bank, they headed south toward

Dundas and Millersburg. The James brothers abandoned the rest of the gang and headed to what is now South Dakota. After many days of searching, by over a thousand men, the others were finally caught at a place called Hanska Slough. They had a gunfight there before they gave up and the survivors were taken to the Flanders House Hotel in Madelia." Looking in the rearview mirror, Bud asked, "Do you want to go to any or all of those places?"

"As I said at the beginning, I want an overview of the whole raid. Let's go!"

So off they went on an extended junket in southwestern Minnesota financed by a Minneapolis newspaper. On the way to Madelia, Lucy signaled Bud to stop at several points along the way so she could take pictures. She was quite chatty during the ride and peppered Bud with questions about life in Northfield, what it was like being a cab driver, and the history of the DJJD celebration. They paid a visit to the Watonwan Historical Society to view pictures of the Flanders Hotel as it existed at the time of the robbery before having lunch at the Triangle Cafe and returning to Northfield.

"It was a nice ride and I got some good pictures," said Lucy as she handed Bud the $50 plus a $5 tip. "And thanks for the commentary about the raid and life in Northfield. I think I'll be able to make a good Sunday Supplement article about your celebration down here. Watch for it!"

Bud plopped himself down on the couch when he got back to the cab office, tired out by the driving and all the talking. "I don't know how you extraverts do it," he said addressing Fat. "It's an effort for me. I just don't have that gift of gab that you folks have."

Fat laughed. "Awrrr. You'll pick it up, Bud, and maybe you'll get to like it. It's just a way to break the ice or feel someone out to see what they think. It's like bull shitting – it sets a tone. You don't always have to be talking about earth-shattering events or great philosophical ideas. People aren't listening to you half the time anyway."

Bud glanced at Fat, then looked away. Maybe that is all that chit-chat is. Maybe that's why they call it "shooting the breeze" or "chewing the fat." He always thought it seemed kind of artificial, like playing a role or being inauthentic. Maybe it had a purpose after all. And maybe he wasn't as bad at it as he had thought. After all, Lucy thanked him for his comments.

***

Milt had taken the day off "to check out the festivities" as had the rest of the gang. They all met at the Odd Fellows picnic area for a final run-through of the plan. The previous night they had procured a couple of dummies from Perman's storage facility, decked them out in hats and shirts to look like hoodlums, and placed them in a stolen cargo van. They drove the van up near the bank cashier's house, parked across the street so it could be seen from the front window or porch.

As they all expected, Billy was as anxious as a dog that had been locked up all day and feared soiling the carpet.

"Oh Jesus!" exclaimed Billy. "What if we get caught? What if the bankers don't comply with our demands? This could all turn bad in the blink of an eye! Maybe we should call it off."

"Just settle down, Billy," said Milt in an authoritative and calming voice. "We aren't going to call it off. We aren't going to get caught as long as we follow the plan. The employees aren't going to resist us for a few dollars as long as they fear for their lives."

Clarence chimed in: "Just get a hold of yourself, Billy. You go through this all the time and nothing has ever come of it. Milt's always kept us on track. Just chill out, for Christ's sake!"

Billy shut up but still showed some residual tenseness evident in shaky hands and inability to stay seated for very long. Everyone ignored him and focused their attention on Milt.

"OK, said Milt. "I see everyone is appropriately dressed as cowboys. Make sure your bandannas are around your necks and they will go up over your nose and not fall off. Do you have your guns and knives?"

Everyone grunted their assent or showed their weapons.

"The re-enactment is scheduled to start at two

o'clock," Milt continued. "We are going to go park our cars behind the Malt O'Meal plant. The rubber boats are tied up down at the old Travelers Park. Howard, I want you to go down and get them and bring them up behind Zanmiller's Sheet Metal Shop as soon as we break up here. We are plenty early so I am allowing half an hour for you to do that. That should give us some wiggle room in case there are any problems getting the boats up there. Des will be there to watch over them until the gig is over. Then you go over to the north side of the bridge and join Billy and Dale who will be leaning against the rail real casual-like, just chatting and looking around, waiting for the raid to start. Once we hear the first gunshots, you three will move to the entrance of the bank. Clarence and I will join you from across the street. Be sure to raise your masks before you enter the bank. Any questions?"

The parties all looked at each other but no one said a word.

"OK then. Let's do it. Remember to stick to the plan and we'll pull this off."

The gang piled into two cars and headed down West Third Street. The car that Howard rode in made a left at Water Street and took him up to the Traveler's Park at the end of St. Olaf Avenue, returning to park at the south side wall of the Crow's Nest, next to the other car. They all got into one car and Milt passed a bottle of Seagram's Seven around.

"Now this is just to settle your nerves and get

you calmed down so you can play the part of cowboy revelers without sticking out too much. We have to keep our heads about us or we could screw this up."

"Ya, boss," said Clarence as he took a healthy swig of the whiskey, passing it on to Billy, who was most in need of a sedative. Dale made a modest draw on the spirits, then, looking out at the somber faces, began to laugh hilariously.

"Look at us! We're going to rob our first fucking bank! Cheer up, for crying out loud. How do you think Dillinger started out? It should be a blast and we're going to get away with it and make all those smug, self-righteous citizens shit tacks!"

Everyone smiled or chuckled. Billy giggled. Clarence guffawed and said, "That's the ticket, Dale! Now we're getting with the program!"

Des came out of the bar and spotted the gang parked along the side of the building. She walked over to Milt's window and smiled.

"Everything on track for an exciting day?" she asked.

"Couldn't be better, said Milt. You headed down behind Zanmiller's?"

"Yeah. Reckon I'll strut down that way. See if the fish are biting!"

"Good girl," said Milt. "We'll see you shortly. Stay cool!"

Dale and Billy took up their positions on the bridge and Howard joined them a few minutes later. They started telling jokes to pass the time and look like they were in light-hearted conversation. Clarence and Milt leaned against the wall of the bar, out of sight of anyone inside. Pretty soon they heard the sound of hoofbeats on the cement roadway as two riders took up positions on the far side of the bridge.

***

Squint Howard was in the little park (actually a wide grassed corridor) near the east side of the river. He was chatting about the quality of the festival compared to early years with his long-time friends, Lonnie Van Gilder and Johnny Olson. It was no surprise that the smell of gin wafted from their perches on the iron benches scattered about the park and their voices were not modulated to fit the occasion. Other festival-goers kept a clear perimeter around the trio.

Lewie Norstad came over from his shop to see the re-enactment. He walked around Bridge Square, said hello to several old customers and friends, acknowledged Squint when their eyes met, and said "How are you doing Squint?"

"As well as can be expected, Lewie. And you?"

"I'm doing really fine, Squint. Seem to have got my act back together with the help of a fantastic partner. Hope you see better days too, my friend."

Combat vets always seem to know other combat vets and implicitly recognize each other's struggles."Yeah. See you. Lewie."

Lewie encountered his wife and young daughter who came downtown to watch the goings-on. He hoisted his daughter onto his shoulders so she could better view the crowd and the upcoming shoot-out in front of the place where the First National Bank used to stand.

John D. Nutting, son of the president of First National Bank of Northfield at the time of the raid, crossed his path. John D. was the current president of the bank and was well-known to most everyone in town. The small, thin, wrinkled, and stooped-over man wearing rimless glasses knew Lewie from all the work the latter had done on appliances in his magnificent three-plus story Victorian house at Third and Union Streets. Lewie introduced him to his wife and daughter.

"You're a lucky man, Lewie Norstad, to have two such beautiful women in your life."

"You betcha!" replied Lewie.

"Say Lewie, why don't you stop by down at the bank one of these days and we can talk about your idea of starting a hunting and fishing guide business. What with your efforts to get a pilot's license, that might be a quite profitable endeavor."

"Thanks, Mr. Nutting. I appreciate it."

The narrator for the re-enactment tapped his microphone to make sure it was working and then announced "Ladies and gentlemen, welcome to the official re-enactment of the raid on the First National Bank of Northfield by the combined Jesse James and Cole Younger bands of outlaws. It was a pleasant fall day in Northfield when these desperadoes rode into town. They had been here for several days, checking out the capability of the community and the character of its citizens to respond to an armed bank raid. Two of them, posing as cattle buyers, dickered with a farmer living a couple of miles outside of town about buying his farm, at the same time inquiring about the temperament of the people in town and their preparedness in the event of an emergency. We don't know what they were told but it seems it fits in with their beliefs about the town when they chose it as a target.

"Many of the bank officials, including the official cashier, George M. Phillips, were in Philadelphia attending the World Exposition. Shortly before 2:00 p. m. the directors had ended a board meeting and dispersed, leaving three employees in the bank: Joseph Lee Heywood, bookkeeper and acting cashier, Alonzo E. Bunker, teller, and Frank J. Wilcox, assistant.

Thirty-nine-year-old Heywood, a New Hampshire native, had been with the bank for four years and had lived in Northfield for nine years. Bunker, 27 years old and also a New Hampshire native, had been with the bank for three years and had a background in the printing business. Wilcox, son of a Baptist clergyman from Massachusetts, had come to Northfield with his parents at ten years of age and was looking forward to his 28th birthday on September 8, 1876. He had been with the bank for less than two years.

"Two of the bandits took up positions over at

the end of the bridge," the narrator continued as he pointed out the two men on horses.

The sounds of horses clomping on the pavement were heard.

"And three other outlaws rode up to the bank and entered. Passing citizens were suspicious of the strangers. J. S. Allen, who operated a hardware store on the square, went to the bank to investigate and was manhandled and threatened by Clell Miller."

The enactors acted out the scene.

"That tipped off all the others that were watching and they sounded the alarm: 'Robbers at the bank!' Then an additional group of three more bandits started riding up and down the street, firing their guns at store windows and telling people to stay off the street."

Three men on horseback rode up and down the street, firing their guns in the air and yelling at the crowds assembled alongside the sidewalks for the show. Shots rang out from local citizens enacting the parts of their 1876 brethren .

13 STICK 'EM UP!

All eyes were turned toward the simulated bank on Division Street when the shots from the re-en-actors were heard. The three men leaning on the rail of the bridge quickly moved toward the State Bank. Milt and Clarence joined them from across the street as they entered the bank.

Milt stood in the doorway with a gun in hand as Clarence barged into the cashier's office, brandish-ing a gun in one hand and a knife in the other.

"This is a stick-up. Keep your mouth shut and don't cause any problems and you won't get hurt. Grab your master key to the safe-deposit boxes and your list of owners and come with me."

Clarence gave the list of safe deposit box owners to Milt, who had told him he needed them to pri-oritize the containers for their search. He did that in a cursory way but actually what he was look-ing for was the box owned by Hermann Schmidt, the one that was supposed to contain thousands of dollars worth of bearer bonds.

Clarence grabbed the cashier, Mr. Harwood, by the arm and pulled him out to the main room where Howard and Milt were holding the tellers at gunpoint with arms raised. Dale worked his way behind the teller windows and warned them not to press any hidden buttons. Then he herded them into the board room where Billy bound their hands, ordered them to sit on the floor, and tied their feet together.

One of the tellers, Becky, thought she saw some familiarity in the walk and mannerisms of one of the bandits and quietly called out, "Is that you Dale?"

All of the other holdup men looked at Dale and then back at the teller who identified one of their mates. Almost in unison, they threatened her into silence.

"Shut your trap, little girl, or I'll come over there and shut it for you," shouted Milt and he stepped toward her and raised his gun hand as if he were about to strike her. Dale did not respond and acted as though he hadn't heard his name mentioned.

Clarence sat the cashier down next to the phone in the boardroom.

"Alright, now I want you to give me the combination to the safe."

"I...I can't do that," said the cashier as he raised his arms to ward off a blow he thought sure would be coming.

"You can if you want to keep your brains inside your skull," said Clarence as he shoved the barrel of his pistol in the face of the cashier. "And don't give me any bullshit about it being on a time lock, either."

"I'll lose my job if I give it to you," pleaded the cashier.

"You'll lose your life if you don't," snarled Clarence.

"And your wife and kid will lose theirs too," chimed in Milt.

"You wouldn't do that. I can't believe anyone would be that cruel," whined the cashier.

"Alright, take that phone and ring up your home. Do it and don't fuck with me. I'll tell you what to say once you have your wife on the line."

The resistant but rattled cashier reluctantly picked up the receiver and dialed his home phone number.

"Hello, honey. I need to ask you to do something for me. Hold the line a minute."

"Ask her to go to the front window and look across the street, down the block aways. Ask her if she sees a white van parked there with two men in it and keep her on the line until I tell you to hang up."

The cashier complied and his wife did what he asked.

"Yes, I see it and there looks like two men are sitting in it, said the bewildered wife of the cashier. "What do they want? Is there something wrong?"

"Thanks, honey. No, it's nothing important. Don't worry about it. I'll tell you about it when I get home. Hold on a minute. I have to check something."

"Those guys are part of our gang," said Milt. Unless they receive a signal from us, they are under orders to go in and rape and beat the shit out of your wife and daughter and rob your house of any valuables. If you don't want that to happen, you better give us the combination right now!"

"OK, OK. I'll do it said the cashier. Now give them the signal so they don't enter the house!"

"Right. The signal is for your wife to go out on the porch and wave her hand back and forth in the direction of the truck. Then go back inside. She is to talk with no one, do you understand?"

The cashier nodded his assent.

"Now tell her to do that. Tell her to talk with no one and stay off the phone in case you need to talk with her again."

The cashier did as he was told. His wife said she didn't understand what was going on but she would do as he wished. Clarence took the phone from him and hung it up.

Unbeknown to the people in the bank, the cashier's wife thought waving at the men in the van was rather odd and sensed that something did not sound quite right. She hailed a neighbor who sent her 12-year-old son out to ride past the parked van on his bicycle. When he did, he saw that the figures in the truck were mannequins with hats on and reported it to his mother who relayed the information back to Mrs. Harwood. Getting more anxious, she called the police.

"Northfield Police. Derwood Attwater speaking. How can I help you?"

"Well, yes. This is Mrs. Harwood, wife of the cashier at the State Bank. I don't know if this is anything to be concerned about but my husband called a few minutes ago and asked me to wave at a van parked down the block. My neighbor's son rode his bike past the van and said it had dummies with hats on sitting in the driver's and passenger's side seats. Don't you think that sounds strange?"

"Yes, it does, Mrs. Harwood. All the officers are busy right now with the festivities going on in the Square. As soon as I can get hold of one of the officers, I'll have him go check it out."

Meanwhile, inside the bank, Milt demanded, "OK. What's the combination?

"Start by going full circle left twice. Then go right to 36...no 38."

"Which is it, asshole? screamed Clarence, as he tried to write down the numbers on a bank deposit slip.

"38. It's 38. Then go left one full turn and land on 14. Then go back right to 4...no to 2. That's it"

Clarence gave the slip with the numbers on it to Howard who entered the open vault and tried to open the safe. Billy tied up the cashier and placed him on the floor next to the tellers.

Clarence took the master key and began unlocking the safe deposit boxes. Milt went through the list of owners and checked off the ones that he knew were owned by prominent people in town. Then he walked along, opening boxes that were checked on his list first, sifting through the contents, and placing what he considered valuable into one of several grocery bags he carried. The box owned by Hermann Schmidt was circled on his list and when he came to it, he dumped the entire contents into the bag that was destined to be "his" to carry out of the bank.

Howard was having trouble opening the safe. He misread the crossed-out numbers on Clarence's deposit slip and had to go back to get clarification of what it was the writer had intended. When that didn't work, he went to the cashier to get him to report the numbers again.

Clarence, getting anxious about the time being wasted and angry at the cashier for dithering on the correct numbers, whacked the cashier along the side of his head with his revolver. The unintended result was that the cashier became dizzy and unresponsive to further demands to fork over the correct numbers.

Finally, Howard got the safe open and grabbed the bundles of cash therein. He dispersed the bundles in five roughly equal heaps on a vault tray and Milt distributed them among the grocery bags he had been filling with safe deposit contents.

Dale maintained a maximal distance from his sister, hoping that she would tell herself and others that it was not her brother who was involved in this robbery. But they continued to make eye contact and both were dismayed that she knew and he knew that she knew the truth. Dale had a hunch that Clarence would shoot her if he was convinced that she would identify all of them and Becky was afraid that might be the result also. So she kept her mouth shut and he kept his distance, played his part, and urged the gang to finish up and get out of the bank.

Milt decided that he had what he was after and that there was enough booty for the gang members to be satisfied with their haul. He distributed the bags to the members of the gang, keeping the one with the contents of Schmidt's box for himself.

"Let's get the hell out of here," Milt proclaimed. "OK. Do as planned. You two walk out of the bank and head for the departure place."

Billy and Dale walked out the door, lowered their masks, and tried to look casual as they made their way to the alley beside Zanmiller's shop.

Milt waited about two minutes and indicated for Clarence and Howard to head to the door. Halfway there, Clarence stopped and with a sneer on his face, raised his pistol and shot the cashier in the head.

"Son of a bitch tried to screw us up on opening the fucking safe. Bastard deserves to die," said Clarence addressing Milt.

"Oh, you dumb shithead! What the fuck have you done! Now we are going to be on the hook for murder and the whole goddamned state is going to be looking for us. Get the fuck out of here before I drop you right now you mother-fucking idiot. I'll take care of things here and join you in a couple of minutes. If I don't show up in five minutes, take off without me. I'll catch up."

Clarence did not expect such a withering rebuke from his hero and, chagrined, he made his way out of the bank. Howard was angry at Clarence too but knew he had to stick to the plan for their escape. He could deal with Clarence later.

When they got to the riverfront behind Zanmiller's, they found Des waiting with one boat. Billy and Dale had already departed down the river. They waited the specified five minutes, then, at Des's urging, got in the boat and headed downstream. When they got to the Second Street bridge, they started their Johnson outboard motor and were propelled rapidly downstream, aided by the rushing Cannon.

Milt was the last one out of the bank. Shaken by the shooting, he forgot to lock the door on the way out. Rather than follow the route of his protégés, he walked across the street to his car parked alongside the Crow's Nest. Des joined him a few seconds later. Tossing his mask and cowboy hat into the back seat, he drove north on Water Street to Second, crossed the bridge, and turned left on Division, heading toward Stanton Airfield. He smiled when he saw the stern of the second boat followed by its wake as he crossed the bridge.

"We did it!" exclaimed Milt. "Goddamn, we pulled it off. Those guys will be happy with their haul. We can get back together again after things cool off."

"Now we got to make it out of the state as soon as we can," said Des. "What an adventure. We're like fuckin' Bonnie and Clyde! Time to celebrate," she said as she leaned over and unzipped Milt's pants, intending to give him some head along the way. Milt didn't object but when he nearly went into the ditch alongside the road, he lifted her head.

"I think we are going to have to save that for later, honey. While we are on the way, why don't you get the bearer bonds and cash out of the grocery bag and put it in the valise in the back seat? We'll put the good jewelry in your suitcase when we stop. "

***

Squint had seen the three men standing on the north side of the cement bridge but was too far away to be able to identify them. Like the others in the crowd, his attention was directed toward the gunfire and horses prancing on the pavement in front of the location of the old First National Bank. When he turned around to have a cigarette after the simulated bank robbers rode off down South Division Street, something didn't seem right to him. Then it struck him that the three men on the bridge were no longer there. He asked his friends, Lonnie and Johnny, if they had seen the three men leaning on the railing but neither of them had been paying attention.

"I think I'll walk over to the other side of the river and see if anything is amiss," he told his companions. Squint traveled at a fast limp, his shrapnel injured leg slowing him down. He looked up and down the street on the north side of Bridge Square as he crossed the bridge but he didn't spot the three men dressed as cowboys. He glanced down the river and thought he saw the wake of a motorboat in the distance. He peered in the windows of the State Bank but saw no human movement. That's odd, he thought.

Rounding the corner, he pushed open the doors to the bank, hesitating somewhat for he had never been inside the building before.

"Hello! Anyone here?" he yelled out as he entered the main lobby and saw no one behind the tellers' cages. Silence. Then he moved toward the board room and heard muffled cries for help. Cautiously, he opened the door and saw the three bound tellers laying on the floor and the body of the slain cashier, laying in a pool of blood.

"Good God almighty," Squint exclaimed as he knelt to remove the gag and untie the ropes from the first teller. "What has happened here?"

"We were robbed by five men. They forced Mr. Harwood to open the safe. They went through all the safe deposit boxes. Then one of them, the biggest and meanest one, shot poor Mr. Harwood in the head. It was horrible!" All three of the tellers were crying.

Squint removed the ropes from Becky. Then he and

another teller unbound the remaining victims.

"Call the police," said Squint as he took command of the situation. "You may not be able to get through to anyone because of the goings-on out there. I'll get out to Bridge Square and sound the alarm. There will be people here to help you very soon. Don't worry the robbers are gone now," he said trying to be reassuring.

Out on the street, Squint did his fast limp across the bridge at the same time yelling "Help, help! They robbed the bank and shot the cashier!"

A member of the crowd, recognizing Squint and thinking he must be drunk, said, " What's that old sot yelling about?"

Another yelled back at him, "Of course, they robbed the bank and shot the cashier. That's what they're supposed to do. They've done it every year since 1948. Sleep if off old-timer."

"No, no! It's real and it's now. Down at the State Bank. Get down there and help those poor girls! They're scared out of their minds!"

Squint spotted Lewie and rushed up to him. "Lewie, I ain't drunk. Believe me. Some bastards just robbed the State Bank and killed the cashier. I think they may have made their escape down the river."

"I believe you, Squint." Putting his daughter down in the custody of her mother and addressing Squint, he said, "You go see if you can find Bob Sletten or one of the other cops. They're all busy right now directing traffic and trying to control this crowd. I'll see if I can find someone to help track and catch them.

Lewie ran down the block to his shop, yelling into the cab stand as he went by that someone had robbed the State Bank and that they were making their escape down the Cannon. He ran into his shop, picked a .30-06 with a new laminated stock off his gun rack, and stuck a box of ammunition in his pocket. Bud and Zack had brought their archery equipment to work, intending to go out to the range after work to get in some practice before the club tournament. They were already on their way up Third Street, bows and arrows in hand, to fetch their motorcycles when Lewie caught up with them.

"There are lots of places where we can access the river. Let's try to catch them at the old Travelers Cabins. If we're too late we can move on downstream to Waterford."

"Gotcha," said Zack as he fixed his equipment to his Zundapp with a couple of rubber bands made from old inner tubes. Bud had fashioned a kind of "quiver" for his arrows on the back fender of his Harley and a pair of clamps on his handlebars for his bow. Lewie put his rifle in the back seat of his old Studebaker and tried to catch up to the two motorcyclists who were already at Second Street.

Zack and Bud got to Pig's Tail Alley in just a couple of minutes and rode to the little cement pad next to a short rock wall on the river bank. One of the rubber rafts had already passed and the second one was coming into view, without engine power, just drifting along with the flow of the river. Billy had flooded the engine and it wouldn't start, causing him to become anxious and frazzled.

"Oh, my god! Oh, my god! Start, goddamn it! We're going to get caught and end up in the slammer. I knew this was a bad idea. Why did we ever listen to Clarence?"

Dale took over the task, pulling the starter cord as fast as he could in an attempt to clear the excess fuel, but to no avail. "Shit, goddamn it! Where are those fucking paddles?" he exclaimed as he searched the bottom of the boat. By that time they were nearly at the tourist park and he could see some movement on the riverbank.

The two archers quickly strung their bows and nocked arrows. Taking aim and leading the boat by about 10 feet, Zack released his broadhead arrow with a "twang" sound as the string hit his arm guard, only to see it sink into the muddy water about a foot short of the boat.

Lewis arrived and took up a position next to Bud. Using a fishing arrow with an attached line, Bud's arrow swooshed to its target, striking the boat midship. A "pop" followed by the sound of air escaping the vessel could be heard as the arrow plowed into the inner spaces of the boat. Bud and Lewis started to pull on the line, drawing the sinking raft closer to shore. The two occupants fired their pistols wildly, it being difficult to take proper aim as they lost their footing and panicked at being dumped into the rushing waters.

Zack nocked another arrow and fired hitting the craft in the stern and causing even more rapid deflation. Both clung to the part of the boat that had not yet lost flotation, their firearms lost in the muddy water. Police arrived and were able to help pull the water-logged desperadoes to shore. In custody, Billy and Dale pleaded for mercy, saying they knew nothing of the murder of Harwood.

Lewie headed for his car and yelled at Zack to join him. "Bring your bow and some arrows. Let's get down to Waterford. Maybe we can catch the other boat there."

14 DOWN THE CANNON

Lewie's tires screeched as his car leaped out of the Tourist Park and made a sharp left to get to Highway 3 going north. Maxing out the three-speed transmission in each gear, Lewie flew over the viaduct, past the Tastee Freeze on the left, and Sheldahl's plastic bag factory on the right. By the time he reached the entrance to the sewage disposal plant he was up over 90 miles per hour and had to begin slowing for the turn off on Highway 47.

"How far up here do you think we should go," asked Zack.

"I think we are ahead of them by a good measure," said Lewie. "What we want is a good position to get a shot at them and stop their boat before they get into territory that isn't close to the road. I think the iron bridge at Waterford is a good bet."

The old eight-panel, single span iron bridge had been built in 1909 to replace an earlier structure at that spot along the Cannon. It was 140 feet long and 16 feet wide resting on concrete abutments.

Lewie parked the car about 20 feet from the end of the bridge so it couldn't be seen because of the trees and bushes growing there. Zack walked across the bridge and took up a position on its southern end. Retrieving his rifle from the back seat of the car, Lewie filled the clip with ammunition and then aimed it upstream, peering through the scope. Nothing in sight yet and just the sounds of birds chirping, bugs and flies buzzing and the occasional fish jumping in the river. The bridge was downstream from a wide northward bend in the river so the boat was likely to be hidden from view up until the last moment.

Lewie went back to the trunk of his car and retrieved a coiled-up length of rope which he tied to one of the bridge girders and placed the coil on the ground next to the bridge. "How about we change places, Zack? That way I can get a longer view upriver since I am equipped for distance shooting while you can take advantage of the short-range action with your bow and arrows."

"Makes sense," said Zack and he walked back over the bridge. "Do you think they'll be shooting at us?"

"Could happen but I think they only have sidearms and it's very difficult to hit anything at a distance with those, especially if you are in a wobbly boat. I have the distance advantage with my rifle."

The pair kneeled on each end of the bridge so as not to present a human profile against the sky. Five minutes passed and then ten. Zack wondered if perhaps they had already passed this point.

What had happened was that the propeller of the second boat had picked up some old fishing line that stopped the engine. They had to stop, pivot the engine and unwind the line, cutting snarls and knots to free it. Clarence moved to the back of the boat to help but just got in the way.

"Dammit, Clarence, just go back to the front of the boat before you dump us into the damn river," snarled Howard as he methodically went about his task. He mumbled something more about "the asshole who shot the cashier and put us all on the hook for a murder charge," but Clarence did not want to hear it, his ears still ringing from the dressing down he received from Milt. Instead, he moved to the front of the boat, sulked, and protested his innocence to some unseen audience.

Zack looked at Lewie, who put a finger to his lips and cupped his left ear to better capture any sounds in the distance. Zack tried cupping his own ear and could hear the faint whining sound of a small-bore Johnson outboard engine. The boat was still not in sight.

Zack watched Lewie survey the waterline through the scope of his rifle. Finally, the barrel stopped moving and he knew that his mentor had a fix on the approaching bandits. Poking his head up a few inches, he could see a black dot on the water flanked by small white wakes on each side.

When the boat was about 200 yards out, Lewie levered a round into the chamber, took careful aim at the outboard engine, and fired. The whining buzz of the engine stopped, the report of the gun echoed over the valley, and birds flew off, frightened by the loud discharge of the .30-06. The occupants of the boat looked confused, at first, then drew their pistols and began to fire ineffectually at the bridge. Lewie chambered another round and fired into the bow of the boat as it slowly drifted toward them and began to imitate the fate of the Titanic. Clarence and Howard instinctively crouched down, not firing their weapons, apparently fearful of drawing any more precision rifle fire. At about 60 yards out, Zack stood up and launched a broadhead at the craft, hitting it just right of center and piercing the rubber hull up to its feathers. Water pushed over the gunwales of the little rubber boat.

"Don't shoot! Don't shoot! I give up," yelled Howard as he threw his gun in the river.

Clarence held onto his weapon, thinking he might still be able to get away somehow.

"Throw down your gun right now," roared Lewie as he stood up and aimed his rifle at Clarence. The latter hesitated and Lewie fired a round into the bottom of the boat between Clarence's knees, causing a fountain of river water to burst upward, soaking the reluctant gunman. Clarence threw away his gun and raised his arms in defeat. Zack took the rope and threw it to the drowning bank robbers.

"Grab onto the rope and I'll pull you over to the river bank." The bedraggled boaters did so, grabbing onto the rushes to pull themselves out of the water. Lewie kept his rifle trained on them, discouraging any sudden moves to try to escape. Zack nocked another arrow and remained at the ready for any change in disposition on the part of the captives.

Three state police cars arrived and disgorged six officers who placed the bank robbers in hand-cuffs and ushered each one into the back of one of the cars. Lewie and Zack pulled the remains of the rubber raft into shore and found two shopping bags filled with water-soaked currency and caches of jewelry, coins, and other small objects. As they turned the loot over to the police officers, they were greeted with pats on the shoulders and grate-ful comments: "Good going guys! Amazing work! Guess any smart-ass punks won't mess with you Northfielders again!"

Lewie and Zack looked at each other with big smiles on their faces. "Guess we make a pretty good team, eh Zack?"

"Oh, Cisco!" said Zack.

"Oh, Pancho!" said Lewie.

They both laughed as they placed their equip-ment in the car and returned to where it all started.

***

Milt and Des drove into the parking lot at the little airstrip in Stanton, Minnesota, about 7 miles from Northfield. In the weeks before the big day, Milt had made preparations for his private refine-ment of "the plan." First, he called on a friend in

Faribault who operated a printing company and also owed him a favor. He inquired about fabricating two sham driver's licenses and passports each for himself and a woman friend who would be posing as his wife. The unscrupulous printer assured him it could be done in about a week if they each could come in for black and white photos.

Once he had these documents in hand, he drove out to Stanton airfield. The little grass airstrip was started by Carleton College in 1942 to train flight instructors for the military. Milt remembered that, after the war, the B-17 that had been flown in for training purposes was actually flown out again, defying the wagers of locals that it couldn't be done.

Milt was sure the owners, Malcolm and Margaret Manuel, didn't know him since they traveled in quite different social circles. He asked if he could charter a Cessna 172 to take him and his wife to Wold-Chamberlain Airport in Minneapolis on September Seventh. The owners assured him they could accommodate his needs if he would put down a small deposit and fill out some papers. Milt did so, under his assumed name and left with a receipt.

Now, the day of the robbery, the couple got out of the car, retrieved two suitcases from the trunk, and made a final inspection of the inside of the car to make sure no incriminating information was left for the federal investigators who they knew would, eventually, check it out. Des put the jewelry she thought was valuable in her suitcase and left the remains in the grocery bag, which she deposited in a trash can next to the building.

"I told them we were going to get a flight in Minneapolis to go to the east coast. They might ask which city so let's say Boston. We're going there for the wedding of your younger brother. Got it?"

"Got it!. Boston. Wedding of my younger brother. Wonder who he's getting hitched to?"

Milt chortled as they walked into the hanger. Mechanics were working on the engine of an old Piper J-3 Cub. Entering the office, they were greeted by Malcolm.

Milt handed him his receipt and said "We're here for a ride to the Minneapolis Airport. Have to catch a flight to Boston."

"Of course, Mr. Henderson. Your aircraft will be ready in just a couple of minutes. Do you want to pay your balance by check or with cash?"

"I'll pay with cash," said Milt as he pulled out some of his newly acquired loot.

"Do you want to use the restrooms before your flight? It will take about half an hour plus some time on the tarmac when you get there."

"Good idea, said Milt as he ushered Des off to the women's room, fearing she might blurt out some comment that could help investigators find them.

Soon they were escorted to the Cessna 172 Skyhawk and their baggage placed in the storage compartment behind the four seats. The noise and vibration of taking off on the grass airstrip caused them to clench onto their seats for a few minutes before they settled into the soft cushion of air supporting them once they got airborne. When they reached cruising altitude, about 2,000 feet, they viewed the harvested farmland below and tried to spot towns and rivers they knew from ground level. Milt was thankful that engine noise made conversations with the pilot difficult.

Inside the terminal at Wold-Chamberlain, named for two pilots who lost their lives in WWI, Milt led Des to the ticket counter for Northwest Airways. Dropping the "Henderson" name, they purchased tickets to Kansas City using their "Richardson" identities. That was part of Milt's diversionary escape plan, for once they got to Kansas City, they would purchase tickets to Houston, Texas, and then to Tucson, Arizona. They would hide out in Tucson while Milt disposed of his bearer bonds and hocked some precious jewelry items. Then, if there were any indications of the law getting close, they could drive the 60 miles to Nogales or fly to Guadalajara.

In Tucson, they had a cab driver take them to a used car lot on Oracle Road where they purchased a 1958 Chevy Impala with Milt's share of the cash from the safe. Driving downtown, they stopped at the El Charro for a lunch of tacos and enchiladas. Milt picked up a newspaper to look for places to stay. After learning from the waiter that the "snow-birds" were beginning to arrive from the north and competition for lodging would soon get fierce, he found a small detached older house on Incas Place available. Driving up the secluded street, he observed that the house was set back from the street by several car lengths with a duplex ahead of it and to the south. It looked like a good place to camp out until they decided to make their next move.

"Won't be the first place anyone would look for us," said Des. "And it's kind of cute tucked in there among some large old trees. Don't find a lot of shade in this part of the country."

The house was furnished enough to be livable. Milt and Des drove over to get supplies from a nearby grocery store on the corner of Grant Road and North First Avenue. They picked up a used TV set at a second-hand store to keep abreast of any news about the bank robbery in Minnesota. After a few days of watching news reports and reading out-of-town newspapers, Milt was satisfied that his escape plan had worked. Only the *Minneapolis Star and Tribune* seemed to have any interest in the Northfield caper; newspapers from other large cities never even mentioned it after the first day and then only because it was ironic that it occurred during the celebration of a robbery some 80 years earlier. It was too bad about the boys being caught on the river and now sitting in the Rice County Jail. But they hadn't yet fingered Milt – good boys to the end, he thought. Police were seeking a "fifth bandit" or person of interest thought to be in the upper Midwest area.

Once settled into their hideout, Milt sat down with Des to go over their proceeds from the robbery. Milt's share of the cash from the safe was $20,000, much more than expected. There was also some jewelry that Des estimated to be worth about $10,000 but they knew they would be able to get only a fraction of that if pawned. Des picked out the pieces with diamonds in them and started to unload them at local pawn shops.

And then there were the bearer bonds. The German Gold Bonds were issued from 1924 to 1930 and denominated in US dollars. Milt estimated that their face value was somewhere in the neighborhood of $200,000. Old Schmidt must have had them salted away for a lot of years or else he had purchased them from a previous owner at a discount. After reading the terms written on the bonds, Milt concluded that they could submit the attached coupons for yearly interest payments of seven percent. The different bonds had different payment dates but yearly they would yield a total of $14,000 per year.

"That's more than twice the average income in the United States," exclaimed Milt. "We're standing in the high cotton, Des baby! But I'd rather get rid of the bonds altogether and have no connection to anything that can be traced to Northfield."

What Milt had to do was convert them to cash in such a way as to not arouse suspicion about how he got them. He figured the way to do that was to disperse his efforts in small amounts over several different banks.

Milt first tried calling Bank of the West and was told by a clerk that they didn't conduct foreign transactions. Obviously, the guy didn't know anything about bearer bonds. Next, he called Pima Federal Credit Union and was told they were a savings and loan institution and didn't involve themselves in the foreign exchange market. Finally, a customer representative at Wells Fargo knew what he was talking about.

"Yes, Mr. Richardson, we might be able to help you out. But you will have to bring the bonds in so we can see just exactly what kind they are. Can you do that?"

Milt hesitated, uncertain if the person he was talking to was aware of the robbery and was just setting him up for an arrest. Finally, he responded. "Yes, I'll bring them in tomorrow about two o'clock."

"Fine. Just go to the new accounts desk and ask for Mr. Wilcox when you get here."

Milt didn't intend to bring all of the bonds in at that first meeting, just enough so that he could tell if it would work. Des would enter the bank at the same time and go through the motions of establishing a savings account. She would be armed and if things went south for Milt, she was to intervene by drawing her gun and holding an employee captive. Milt would then draw his pistol and the two of them would rob the teller's windows before making their getaway, all in true Bonnie and Clyde style.

Milt walked slowly into the bank, quickly surveying the activity of the employees and the few patrons present. Nothing seemed amiss. He asked for Mr. Wilcox and soon a bespectacled bald man appeared with outstretched hand and introduced himself.

"Come into my office. You brought the bonds, I presume?"

"Yes, some of them," Milt said as he handed the man a manila envelope containing three bonds in the amounts of one, five, and ten thousand dollars. "I inherited the bonds from my father's estate when he died a few weeks ago."

"Oh, I'm sorry for your loss, Mr. Richardson. Now let's see what we have here. H'm. Gold-backed German bearer bonds. I haven't seen any of these in quite a few years. Back in the roaring twenties, Americans bought millions of dollars worth of these that Wall Street marketed on Germany's behalf so they could pay off their World War I reparation obligations. When Hitler took over in 1933 they defaulted and wouldn't honor these bonds"

Shaken, Milt blurted out, "What, you mean these bonds are worthless?"

"Well, it's complicated," said Mr. Wilcox. "In 1951 Germany said they would honor their debts by replacing these bonds with newer ones at a reduced value but there was a catch. They claimed the Russians had looted millions of these bonds from their vault at the end of the war. So they demanded that holders of these bonds prove that their bonds were not in Germany in 1945 and could not have been stolen by the Russians."

"How can you prove anything like that?" asked Milt.

"That's the thing," said Mr. Wilcox. "Nobody had that kind of proof. So in 1953 international officials reached an agreement, called the London Debt Accord, that included a scheme where holders of the bonds could exchange for new bonds that paid half the original coupon, or 3.5%. The US. officials successfully lobbied to have written into the accord an option that debt holders could hang on to their old bonds, collect the 3.5% interest, and petition to sell them, but they would have to wait 41 years to do it — enough time for Germany to pay off the reissued debt. And that grace period won't end until April 1994. "

"What the hell," said Milt. "That's not right"

"No, it's not," said Wilcox. "What Germany did was to sweep their pre-World War II debt under the rug and the government and Wall Street went along with it. It will catch up with them eventually, but for the short term, the holders of these bonds have to settle for a 3.5% return and can't cash out their bonds."

"Oh, shit. Goddamn it," exclaimed Milt. "I've got a lot of these. What am I going to do? This was supposed to be my inheritance."

"You say you have a lot of them?" asked Wilcox. "What do you think is the total value?"

"About $200,000," said Milt.

"How long have you had them?" asked Wilcox, angling to find out how much this person knew about bearer bonds.

"I just got them a few weeks ago when my dad died," Milt lied.

"And you haven't done anything with them since that time?"

"No. I thought I could cash them in at any time."

Wilcox began to wonder about the veracity of his client's story of how he acquired the bonds. Maybe they were stolen, he thought. Even so, there was no way to trace them so it would be safe to acquire them. Just how eager is he to get rid of them, he wondered?

"Hold on," said Wilcox. "There might be something we can do. Let me go talk to my superior a minute. I'll be right back."

Milt was upset by this turn of events as he was fidgeting in his chair, mumbling under his breath, tapping his feet on the floor. What the fuck, he thought. Don't tell me I got snookered on this deal. Des could tell Milt was upset and reached inside her purse, fingering her revolver.

Soon Wilcox returned. "Well, my boss says the bank isn't interested in holding German Gold Bonds for thirty years for a mere 3.5% return on the investment before they can be redeemed. But I tell you what, you might be able to recover some money from these bonds if you sell them at a significant discount. It means sacrificing a good deal of the face amount of the bonds but it could provide you with a significant amount of cash in hand."

"How much of a sacrifice are we talking about?" asked Milt.

"I know a guy, he's not with this bank, who might give you 15 percent of the face value," said Wilcox. "Ordinarily, people can be expected to double their money every eight years on an investment but this is an especially risky one given that a foreign government is involved and the interest rate is fixed. But this guy is pretty well off and might be able to hold onto the bonds for a while or he may be able to trade them for something else within his network of associates."

Wilcox wasn't being entirely straightforward with Milt. If his friend bought the bonds for $30,000 he could make 23% interest per year, totaling $238,000 for the 34 years plus he could then cash in the bonds and receive another $200,000 for a total of 43% gain per year on his initial investment. And he wasn't saying who this friend was and who his associates were.

"That's one hell of a sacrifice," said Milt, smelling a rat. "I think I'll have to get back to you on this."

Milt went back to his rental house and told Des what had happened. "The asshole is trying to dupe me into selling the bonds at a huge discount. The greedy bastard wants to screw me over and make a bundle for this fucking friend of his. I aught to burn his fucking house down!"

"Wait a minute, Milt," said Des. "We could just hold onto the damn things and collect the seven grand interest each year. That's more than most people make and we could keep a low profile."

"Yeah, but we'd have to travel around to different banks to redeem the coupons in case some smart FBI agent decides to check banks for any unusual traffic in bearer bonds. It gets to be too much of a hassle. Maybe I can talk this guy into giving me a better deal."

The next morning, Milt called Wilcox and said he would like to meet with his friend and discuss the possible transaction. Wilcox told Milt he would call him back in a few minutes. When he did, he told Milt to go to Luigi's Italian Delicatessen on Speedway at 11:00 and ask for Mr. B.

15 TRY THE CANNOLI

The delicatessen was a good sized store in a new building with contemporary architecture and parking in the front. Milt's senses were struck with the fragrances of Italian sausages, tomato sauce and espresso coffee when he walked in the door. His mouth began to water as he viewed the cannoli and other exotic pastries behind the glass cases. There were a few small tables with red and white checkered tablecloths draped over them. One was occupied by an older gentleman smoking a cigar and sipping on a cup of espresso. Milt walked up to the waiter at the counter.

"I'm supposed to meet a Mr. B here at 11:00."

The waiter did not speak but indicated with a head nod that it was the distinguished looking white haired gentleman at the table. Milt walked over.

"You Mr. B?" asked Milt.

"Just call me Joe. You Richardson?" asked the man.

"Yeah, that's me," said Milt.

"Sit down and have a coffee. Maybe you want a sandwich. They got good pastrami here or meatballs."

"Yeah, maybe I'll have a salami sandwich and a cup of coffee." He went up to the counter and ordered and then returned to the table.

"You new in town, Mr. Richardson?" asked Joe.

"Yeah. Me and the wife just got here a few days ago. Looking for a new place to settle down."

"That accent sounds like you're from Minnesota," said Joe.

Milt never thought about having an accent and was a bit taken aback by the stranger's observation but decided not to try to hide his origin. After all, a lot of Midwesterners fled to Arizona to avoid the winters.

"You betcha," said Milt, exaggerating the speech of his Scandinavian ancestors. "Came down here to thaw out," he laughed.

"Did you know Kid Cann up there in Minneapolis?"

"I didn't know him. I frequented one of his bars though. He just got nailed for taking a girl across state lines for one of his massage parlors."

"Yeah. Too bad about that. He needs to learn how to keep a low profile."

"Your accent suggests you didn't grow up here either – maybe the old country by way of New York?" said Milt.

Joe laughed too. "I guess you got me there." Shifting to the business at hand, he said, "Wilcox tells me you have a bunch of bearer bonds you want to unload."

"That's right. He told me you might be interested in buying them at a discount. He said 15% but I was hoping you could go a little higher."

"He did, did he? I was thinking about 10%. You can't get rid of those German bearer bonds. All I'd do with them is try to peddle them to one of my business associates at a discount too. I have to have enough leeway to make it worth my while. Kapish?"

Kapish? The setting, the accent, the use of words gave Milt the uneasy feeling that he was talking with someone who was "well-connected." Perhaps a little more deference was in order.

"I don't mean any offense," said Milt. "But I just learned about the difficulty with these bonds from Wilcox. It came as a great shock to me to learn that they aren't easily cashed in. I had plans and now they are all up in the air."

"You say you got them from your father?" asked Joe. "Are you sure you didn't acquire them in another way?"

"Well, some friends might have helped me get them but they are still the property of the bearer. They can't be traced."

"Uh huh," said Joe with a smirk on his face. "You got a job, Mr. Richardson or whatever your name is?"

"Just call me Milt. No, I haven't. I used to run a bar. I had hoped to start a business with the money from the bonds."

"I see," said Joe. "I've had a number of businesses over the years – coat manufacturing, laundries, cheese suppliers, a pasta factory, a trucking company, even some funeral homes. Most of them were back east but I have some things I do here in Tucson too. I consider myself a venture capitalist. Maybe I can find a place for you or maybe I can help you set up that business you were dreaming about. If I gave you 20 or 30 Gs for those bonds, we could get you started and I could be a silent partner. How does that sound to you, Milt?"

"Gee, I don't know," said Milt. "That's not what I expected from this meeting. It's a lot to think about. I'd have to talk it over with my wife. I'm not sure she wants to stay in Tucson."

Seeing that Milt had finished his sandwich, Joe said, "Hey, you gotta have one of those pistachio cannoli for desert" as he signaled the waiter to bring one over to the table.

Milt rolled his eyes as he tasted the cheese-filled pastry. "Wow, that is really delicious!"

Joe said, "Eh, see I don't steer you wrong. Now how about this: Why don't you come to work for me on a part-time basis for a while. I could have you run some errands for me around town and have you take some trips to deliver or pick up special shipments out of town. That way we can see if we can work together and develop some trust. What d'ya think?"

"I think it is worth considering," said Milt. "Let me get back to you tomorrow. Do you have a phone number where you can be reached?"

Joe signaled a burley man sitting at another table to come over. "This here is Pete, my driver. He'll stop by your place tomorrow afternoon and pick you up. That's up on Incas Place isn't it? Bring your wife along and we'll meet at the Kon Tiki for one of their wonderful rum drinks. It's a great place to get out of the hot sun."

Milt was taken aback that Joe already knew where he lived and was disconcerted at the pace this new relationship was taking. This guy sounded like an old Mafiosi but what was he doing in Tucson? This wasn't their usual territory. And what did he want with me, a nobody in the criminal world? It didn't make much sense. He replayed the encounter to Des, who agreed it was strange but at the same time it was exciting and could provide opportunities that would not ordinarily come their way. This could be Milt's chance at the big time.

Pete showed up on time and took the couple down to the restaurant and bar on East Broadway inspired by the 1947 expedition of a balsa wood raft across the Pacific. Joe was already sitting in a bamboo sided booth with palm fronds overhead, looking at the drink menu.

"Come join me," Joe beckoned with a wave. "You two should get a Scorpion Bowl. It is fantastic, made with several kinds of rum, brandy, gin, liquors and tropical fruit juices. You sip it through these long straws and the flavors change as you work your way down to the bottom. I'm going to have a Zombie and I'll get us a Pu-Pu plate too." He ordered the drinks as Des and Milt sat down.

"So this is the misses," said Joe as he surveyed Milt's companion dressed in shorts and a light-weight cotton shirt. "Have you two been together for a long time?"

"Yes, we grew up together in the same town. We've been hanging out together for a lot of years," said Des.

"Up in Minnesota, I suppose. Say, did you hear about that bank robbery up there? A really bold caper, you got to admire that. Did it when the town was celebrating a Jesse James robbery back in the 1800s. That's really cool! Too bad the four bandits got caught. Guess they are still looking for a fifth one but he seems to have disappeared into the northern woods someplace."

Des and Milt made eye contact, both of them knowing that Joe probably knew who they were. But Milt just said no, he hadn't heard about it. And Des chimed in, saying, "Wow. That must have really been something."

"Did Milt explain to you what I have offered him?"

"Yes, but it's still not clear to me what exactly he'll be doing and what he will get out of it," said Des.

"Well we still have to work that out. Maybe we could find a place for you too. You look like the kind of girl that knows her way around. Have you ever supervised others in a business, you know like in a restaurant or bar or a massage parlor?"

"No, I've pretty much worked on my own but I'm willing to learn."

"That's the spirit," said Joe.

And so, Milt and Des began their apprenticeship in organized crime. Both of them obtained Arizona Drivers Licenses to use as valid identifications and they put money down on a house in a new development across from the Rialto Race Track to validate their status as solid citizens. Milt would pick up packages at various locations and deliver them to mysterious places in the desert or in Sabino Canyon. Sometimes he would travel to New York to pick up bundles of cash that he would hide in secret compartments in his luggage. Des would learn the massage parlor business and managed to make some suggestions for new services that increased income by a significant amount. Sometimes the two of them would pose as tourists to Nogales, Mexico where they would stay at the El Camino Hotel, frolic in the pool and buy drinks from the pool-level bar. They would go to The Cave restaurant in Nogales, where they met with representatives of Mexican drug cartels to arrange shipments of drugs across the border and cash or firearms to go in the other direction. Joe B. liked their moxy, their style, and decided to give them the 15% for the bearer bonds, allowing Milt to get a liquor license and open a bar in Tucson. The "fifth man" was realizing his dream at last.

***

Back in Northfield, Zack, Bud and Lewie were being feted for their parts in capturing the desperadoes. The City Council decided to have a gala event for the heroes of the day but they all refused to attend unless Squint was included amongst their number. Some of the councilors resisted, claiming that Squint was nothing but a drunk and embarrassment to the community. But the mayor disagreed, making a moving speech that extolled the virtues of Squint for his valor in WWI , for helping to track down the culprits, and for notifying Lewie of what had happened at the bank. After that speech, anyone calling for Squint's exclusion from the celebratory events was regarded as a pariah in the community.

In the cab office, it was a mixture of adulation and good-natured ribbing for Zack and Bud. Both of them were somewhat embarrassed by all the attention, especially of that from all the citizens who never had a word for them when they were mere cab drivers. Old familiar passengers were full of questions about the chase and whether or not they were frightened. Some customers wished to be driven by one of the two eminent cab drivers but were disappointed when Fat told them drivers were assigned in order of precedence. Both sought the advice of Lewie who just smiled and said, "This too shall pass. Enjoy it for the moment, boys."

The ceremony took place in Bridge Square. Representatives of the bank and the community gave speeches and the Fabulous Four were presented with plaques. Even Fat Lloyd was called upon to say some good words for the men in his employ. Lewie and Squint, having been commended for their actions in wars by generals, were not as excited as the younger generation, but were pleased nevertheless. Squint was in high spirits that his colleagues, Lonnie, Johnny, and Aaron had a peer to cheer on. Lewie was gratified that his daughter, Teri, should see her dad honored by the community. Some local businessmen took up a collection for Bud to ensure the completion of his first year of graduate school or get him to a Peace Corps Training Center, whichever was in his future.

Everyone was pretty sure the fifth bank robber was Milt Grubbs, although none of the captured thieves gave up his name. Many patrons of the Crow's Nest reported that they had seen Milt associate with the four individuals now cooling their heels in the Rice County Jail. He did not show up for work after the robbery and he and his consort, Desiree Goodlove, had both disappeared without a trace. The FBI had put out a "person of interest" notice to local law enforcement agencies seeking his whereabouts but so far had only received the usual "phantom sightings." After about a month, the maintenance men at Stanton Airfield reported an abandoned vehicle parked next to the hanger to the Northfield Police. They ran the license plates and determined it belonged to Milton Grubbs.

FBI agents working the case descended on the owner of the airstrip to go over records of who had flown out of Stanton about the time of the robbery. Seizing on the charter by the mysterious Mr. and Mrs. Henderson, they determined that the couple fit the description of Milt and Des and that they had flown to Wold Chamberlain on the day of the robbery. However, the trail of that name went cold from that point. They could have flown to any airport in the United States using some other name. The FBI interviewed travel agents from all the airlines operating in Minneapolis but were unable to establish credible equivalence between the "Hendersons" and any other couple departing from that airport.

Northfield police interviewed the elder Mr. Grubbs, deeply chagrined by his son's apparent criminality, and anyone else who knew Milt to see if he had ever mentioned anything about a desired location. They went through all his possessions left at his apartment or in his childhood home trying to turn up some clue as to his whereabouts but came away empty-handed. The only photo of the alleged bank robber was taken with a Baby Brownie camera many years earlier and was of questionable resemblance to the Milt of recent years. However, it was turned over to the FBI, reproduced on a circular, and distributed to field offices all over the country.

Becky and her parents were all embarrassed by the involvement of Dale in the robbery. Their shame led them to keep a low profile and avert their eyes whenever his name came up. They didn't show up for the "hero" ceremony and managed to be elsewhere when Zack came calling on Becky.

Zack did not hold her responsible for her brother's behavior but, since his brush with death, he had been thinking more about the brevity of life and the importance of seizing fleeting opportunities when they arose. In this case, it was not a matter of grasping some attractive option before it evaporated but terminating a relationship before it became so locked in by expectations that it would be impossible to escape without causing considerable distress and regret.

Zack had come to the conclusion that he and Becky were not right for each other. They were of different temperaments that would likely clash over the long run rather than make up for each other's deficits. That had already happened but he had "pulled his punches" so that she never knew he was hurt by her remarks.

Now he had the difficult task of how to present it to her. There were self-imposed constraints on how he could solve this problem. Because he was of an empathic and sentimental sort, he did not want to hurt her feelings or validate any sense of shame she was already experiencing. And he didn't want to have to counteract the kind of hostile defensive attack of which he knew she was capable. That would only lead to a nasty dispute filled with bitterness and hostility. He wished they could still be friends afterwards but he would settle for a lack of active detestation. He knew he couldn't just avoid the issue or delay confronting it, for her flawed intuition would surely run amok – she would make of it something that wasn't there.

Zack asked Lewie what he should do. Lewie presented that half smile he used when he was going to be serious.

"Zack, my boy, you are dealing with one of the most difficult problems to face the male gender. Probably no matter how you approach it, she is going to try to make you feel guilty for having abandoned her and taking advantage of her sexually. She will accuse you of infidelity and deception. She won't let you off the hook, no matter how much she had to do with it. You just have to stick with your guns and ride it out. Don't give in to her pleading or you will be sunk forever. It'll be a rough ride but you can handle it."

Believing he deserved a break, Zack basked in his recently acquired notoriety for a few days. Then he decided it was time to get it over with and level with Becky about the way he felt. He called and made a date for lunch at a place far enough away from the scrutiny of nosy Northfielders yet not so far as to have a long uncomfortable ride home after breaking the news. He chose Rosie's Bar and Grill in Farmington, a place that he knew had booths far enough away from the clatter of the lunch counter and kitchen so they could have a decorous conversation.

Becky made idle chatter on the 15 minute ride north on Highway 3. She inquired about how he was enjoying his celebrity and told him how angry she and her parents were at Dale for having allowed himself to get involved with Milt and fancy a criminal life for himself.

"It is just crazy," Becky said. "I mean how could he be so dumb as to think he could get away with a bank robbery, especially one where I worked. He must have known I'd spot him. And he gave no consideration to us, for the way it would affect us. Jesus! He is just an irresponsible jerk and deserves what he gets. And that sonofabitch Clarence is just a devil, a slimy no good bastard, shooting poor Mr. Harwood in the head the way he did. You know Milt was the slime-ball that planned the whole thing, don't you, him and that blond-haired slut that hung around the bar?"

"Yes, I know," said Zack. "The FBI is trying to track them down. They might be in a different country by now."

"The bank manager and the agents are going over what was lost from the safe-deposit boxes," said Becky. "They might be able to trace some of the jewelry if it gets pawned. The agents were questioning me a lot about my brother and at first they thought I might have been in on it, but my boss stood up for me, said I was trustworthy and dependable, so they gave up that line of inquiry. I guess there were a lot of bearer bonds missing from one of the safe-deposit boxes. Since they don't have any registered owner, they can be disposed of without giving your name, so they will be hard to find."

"They didn't find any of those in the stuff retrieved from the ones we caught," said Zack. "'Course, they could be at the bottom of the Cannon or in Lake Byllesby by now."

When they entered the bar and grill, Zack pointed at the most distant booth when the waiter came up to seat them. Zack ordered a grilled cheese sandwich and coffee. Becky ordered a BLT and a glass of milk.

Zack waited until after they had eaten their sandwiches before broaching the subject of their relationship.

"Becky, I've been thinking a lot about us, our relationship, since I piled my motorcycle up on Bridge Square."

Becky stiffened and stared at Zack intently. "Yes, and what is it that you've been thinking?"

"Well, I think we are not really meant for each other. I think we have different outlooks that don't mesh together so well."

"It's because of my brother isn't it? You think I knew what that gang was up to and didn't say anything, so now you're going to get even!"

"No, no, Becky. That isn't it. I know you aren't responsible for what your brother does. I know you and even your parents had no control over him."

"Well what is it, then? Haven't I been nice to you. Didn't I give you my body to enjoy? Aren't I pretty enough for the great big hero in town?"

Zack could tell this wasn't going the direction he had hoped for. She was already in attack mode and he was getting nervous. He could feel her fear and self-loathing and it was making him sick to the stomach because he had been the one to pre-cipitate it.

"No, Becky, you are pretty and you have been nice to me. And I gave my body for you to enjoy too, so it wasn't a one-way street as far as that goes. No, it is that we see things from a different vantage point, have different ways of operating. You are a practical, organized person who wants to plan and be in control of things. I am a more spontaneous person who likes to play it by ear, follow my in-spirations, have variety in life, and judge things by how they feel to me, not because they're logical or expedient. I think we would rub each other the wrong way over time."

"What's wrong with being practical? You can't go chasing your dreams all your life! And what's wrong with planning and being in control? That's the way you achieve goals. You can't just follow all your whims and hope to accomplish something in life! And what's wrong with logic? You have to be objective and logical when you make decisions, you can't just choose something because it makes you feel good."

"There isn't anything wrong with all those

things you mentioned. But that isn't all there is to life. I like to make people feel good and I dislike hurting their feelings. That's why I avoid conflict and try to get people to work out their difference. When I am following an inspiration, I'm euphoric and feel on top of the world. I like the possibilities for the future not just what has always been. Planning is important for some things but I like to stay open to the novel and unexpected. You never know where it might lead you."

"So what are you, some kind of mammy-pamby wuss? Do you like boys more than girls, is that it?"

"No. Becky, I'm not queer. I like girls as sexual partners. I'm not a wimp either. I know how to fight and have done so when it was important. In fact, I've hurt some guys pretty bad. I'm not proud of that and wish it could have been different. I'm just not one of those macho yo-yos that goes around bragging about how tough he is and how he's the world's biggest stud. I'm a peaceable type that likes people to get along."

"So I guess you didn't like it when I took the assertive role down at that motel in Faribault?

"That was fine. I like sexually assertive women. But I would like them to be a little flexible and allow me to make some of the moves, not to control everything. There should be some give and take, or taking turns, whatever."

Becky and Zack were both silent as they drove back to Northfield. Becky saved her last salvo for the very end, when they parked in front of her house.

"I had a feeling you were going to dump me. I could tell you weren't as thrilled with me as you used to be. I suppose you already have someone else you're sleeping with. Well, I'll tell you, you no good sonofabitch, I've got somebody else too. I've been fucking Charley Weldon for months and he proposed to me." Opening the door to leave, she said, "So you can take your effete pecker and put it where the sun doesn't shine!"

Zack was nonplussed. How could she be so spiteful? He had had a taste of it before when she raged against her brother. Lewie had warned him but he didn't think there would be this much vindictiveness.

Finally he mustered a response, "I wasn't unfaithful to you, Becky."

Her jaw dropped and her face reddened. Then she whirled about and ran to the house.

Zack sat there for a few minutes, then slowly drove down to his loft above the fire engines.

16 EPILOGUE

It has been six decades since the events of the State Bank robbery unfolded in Northfield, Minnesota. The face of the town has changed considerably. The taxi cab offices are long gone, replaced by Uber and Lift drivers and government-sponsored transportation for the disabled. There is no longer a Perman's clothing store, a Marshall's dry goods store, an Ice Cream Shop, an Ideal Cafe, a White Castle, or a Jacobsen's Department Store. The Corner Bar was rechristened as a pub and then, in a more recent incarnation, remodeled to artfully expose some of its original construction. Dundas Dine and Dance (3D) no longer graces the entrance to Dundas. The number of gas stations has declined substantially but a few retain their original locations. Anderson Furniture Store and Hughes and Heckler Hardware have been replaced with apartments and the Froggy Bottoms Bar and Restaurant. The Northfield National Bank building was replaced with a modern bank building that is out of character with the rest of downtown. Even the venerable Tiny's has disappeared after being run for many years by one of Tiny's mentees. It is unknown if there is a replacement for the social functions that Tiny's provided for the community.

New storefronts and businesses have appeared along Division Street and the stretch of Highway 3 between Northfield and Dundas has burgeoned with fast-food chains, motels, apartments, and a huge grocery store. The Grand movie theater (originally Ware Auditorium) is now an event center often used for weddings. The old Stuart Hotel was refreshed and renamed the Archer House before it burned down. City fathers are debating what is to replace it. City Hall is now an art gallery and the Police Department has a new home with the Fire Department on West Fifth Street. The old iron bridges on Second Street and Fifth Street have been replaced with low-slung cement structures. The town has nearly doubled in population and is still amazingly viable while other rural communities struggle to survive. Properties once on the edge of town have now been enveloped by residential construction. One large tract, the former home of a St. Olaf English professor, hidden from the road by a perimeter of trees and brush, is giving way to subdivision and diversified housing.

Yet many of the old structures remain. The majority of the buildings along Division Street between Second and Sixth Streets have had no more than face-lifts since the nineteenth century. The Scriver Building on Bridge Square is now home to the Northfield Historical Society and that organization has reclaimed the part of the building that was the original First National Bank and later the 112 Taxi Stand. The old cement bridge on Fourth Street has been refurbished and the State Bank building has been reconditioned to near its original glory, now inhabited by law offices. The old Ben Franklin "dime store" is host to a new business but the building, topped by the round turret on the corner, is the same. John Nutting's Victorian house on Third and Union Streets, with its 37 walk-in closets, trap doors, and crawl spaces in the walls, still proudly stands across from the old Northfield High School, both now owned by Carleton College. Nutting's two daughters gave the house to the college to use as the president's residence after John D. died in 1968.

Bridge Square with its monument, the place where Zack crashed his motorcycle, is mostly the same although there are plans for changing it as well as the little park alongside the river and dam. The *Northfield News* is still printed but without the quaint perspective of Maggie Lee, who spent 68 years chronicling the lives of Northfield persons of interest until her death at age 92. Maggie was an indefatigable newspaperwoman who worked for the enhancement of the community. She also served on several local boards and was a member of statewide journalism organizations. She was awarded the President's Citation by the Minnesota Newspaper Association. The Cannon River still floods, on occasion.

The colleges, St. Olaf and Carleton, have added

many new buildings, grown their student bodies and faculty, and become more expensive while drawing a more diverse assortment of students than in earlier years. St. Olaf has purchased or been given all of the houses on the block leading up to it and are in the process of demolishing the stately old homes (most of which were always used for student housing) in favor of mass student residences, thus taking them off the tax rolls, to the dismay of many of the locals.

The Defeat of Jesse James Days continues to be celebrated every year in Northfield, now bringing over 150,000 people to the event annually. The festivities are well-publicized throughout Minnesota and the reenactments have become more and more elaborate. Performances have even been staged in some foreign countries where interest in the American "Wild West" is great.

Most of the characters that played a part in the drama portrayed in the previous pages have lived out their lives. Fat Lloyd's penchant for cigarettes and coffee did him in at the age of 66 years. He had been waiting for an airplane carrying his brother to the Minneapolis-St. Paul Municipal Airport when he had a massive heart attack and died one year after the death of his mother. His friendliness and colorful story-telling reside in the memories of all the young men who benefitted from his mentoring as they became cab drivers.

H.E. 'Pop' Jones died at the age of 98 after many years of retirement.Consolidation reduced the local cab companies to only one, at which point Pop joined Fat at 777, sharing the dispatching duties of the company. Business continued to drop as the population became more affluent, more college students had cars, the colleges provided more services on campus that used to be provided by local businesses, and drivers became hard to recruit. Subsequent attempts to make taxicab transportation a viable business failed and now there are none.

Harold Grant will be batting no more flies in front of his business next to the old cab office. He died of cardiac arrest after surgery and was buried in his beloved red firefighter's dress jacket. He had served for 29 years for the volunteer fire department, across the street from his business. The sparing partner of Laura Baddgor also wore his Lions Club emblem, after being a 50-year member..

The trench coat man turned out to be the ne'er do well son of a Dundas matron. He always fantasized himself a detective and acted out the role to those who were likely to fall for the ruse. No one knew what he actually did for a living. He was killed when the rail car he was riding in jumped the tracks just south of Farmington.

Argo (aka Lars Kindem) and the members of the Fubar association maintained their friendships for seven decades. One of them, Wayne Quist, compiled many letters that Argo had written to Donny Clark over the years and published them as a memorial to his friend and the group. The book,

GERALD OTIS

called *Dear Donald,* evokes the flavor of the time, place, and individuals who populated Northfield in the 1950s.

Fat Freddy Ferguson became a fishing guide in northern Minnesota during the summers and Florida during the winters. He continued to do "wild and crazy things" with his friends up until he was in his 60s when medical problems curtailed some of his antics. The local constabulary, in collaboration with corrupt mental health providers, a biased judge, unsympathetic relatives, evil guardians, and inept nursing homes managed to kill him by neglect, apparently with no regret. He was missed by many friends who appreciated his "outrageous" pranks, off-beat humor, and astute insight into the foibles of social institutions.

Laura Baddgor died at 87 years and it was noted in her obituary that she "for a long number of years helped keep the Northfield city government on the straight and narrow path." Her coterie of admirers followed her when the Whie Castle was torn down. She took over the Jesse James Cafe in the Scriver Building and local businessmen continued to have a place to congregate, debate politics, or just enjoy the banter.

Professor Rossing was still active at 92 years of age. He wrote over 400 articles and 17 books. He studied ancient Chinese bells from the time of Confucius in various museums and in China he gave a lecture in the city of Wuhan commemorating the tenth anniversary of the discovery of a renowned set of bells that was found in the tomb of the Marquis of Zeng. He also studied sounds made by various violins and studied the acoustics of concert halls, applying what he learned to concert hall design. He received the Gold Medal in Acoustics and the Silver Medal in Musical Acoustics, the Millikan Medal recognizing teachers of physics, and the Rayleigh Medal from the Instituto Mexicano de Acustica.

John D. Nutting was president of the First National Bank and served as a trustee of Carleton. College. The two Nutting daughters, Helen and Ruth, graduated from Carleton in 1940 and 1942, respectively. After John and Elizabeth Nutting died in the late 1960s, the Nutting daughters gave their home to Carleton College for use as a residence for its presidents.

Squint Howard had to have the toes on his left foot amputated when he passed out in a snowbank one evening after a heavy round of drinking with his friends. While he lost his toes and had difficulty walking, the alcohol content of his blood probably saved his life. The city, in one of its compassionate gestures, provided him and his pal, Lonnie, rocking chairs to place out on the sidewalk in front of the Crow's Nest Bar so they could watch the cars go by. Four other men that Tiny Johnson designated as "local characters" died of carbon monoxide poisoning while trying to keep warm with a kerosene heater one winter evening because the gas in the house they occupied had been turned off for nonpayment.

Lewie Norstad completed his pilot's license and was being financed by John Nutting to establish a fly-in fishing and hunting guide business. His plans were cut short when he died from a heart attack at the age of 40 while bow hunting in McGrath Game Refuge. After Lewie died, the archery business in Northfield was taken over by Willy Wolf, who had moved his shoe repair business up the street next to the Ideal Cafe from its original location in Harold Grant's building.

Clarence Dixon was convicted of first-degree murder and served 10 years at the state prison in Stillwater. His surliness and stupidity did not serve him well in prison, especially with some of the older inmates who controlled dispersement of favors. Eventually, he treated another inmate with contempt and was stabbed for his impudence while taking a shower, dying at the age of 35.

Dale Halverson, Howard Kinlaw, and Billy Griffin each spent 5 years in Stillwater before being paroled. Dale eventually moved to Wyoming where he played an outlaw in a wild west show. He ended up working on a ranch as a cowhand until he froze to death when his horse stumbled and crushed Dale's leg during a snow storm. He couldn't walk and was 20 miles from the nearest human outpost.

Howard obtained his bachelor's degree while incarcerated and went on to graduate school when he was released from prison, becoming an electrical engineer. He moved to Florida and worked for Honeywell on servo-mechanisms for the space program, living to the age of 86.

Billy enjoyed only a brief period of relative freedom on parole before he was shot from a passing car by the son of Hermann Schmidt while walking down Main Street in Hastings, Minnesota. Hermann's son obsessed about the robbery and convinced himself that Billy was responsible for the loss of his inheritance, i.e., his father's reputed fortune in bearer bonds. He was apprehended soon afterward, convicted of murder, and served 20 years behind bars at Stillwater.

In 1963, Joe B made plans to assassinate several rivals on the board of an organization he headed in New York. The person he entrusted to carry out the mission betrayed him, however, and the angered board members sought revenge. Joe fled out of the country, turned upon by his mob (who felt abandoned) as well as the other board members. But Joe returned in 1964 only to be kidnapped before he could testify before a grand jury. The board members allowed him to live as long as he stayed in Tucson with his family and didn't try to interfere with their organization's businesses. He was indicted in the late 1970s after one of his "capital ventures" turned into a witness for the FBI. In 1983 he served 8 months for obstruction of justice and in 1985 he did 14 months for contempt of court. A colorful character with some knowledge of classic literature, Joe B made TV appearances and gave interviews to reporters who wrote books about him. His over-inflated ego lead him to write his autobiography. He died of heart failure at the age of 97 in 2002.

Joe B helped Milt Grubbs climb the ladder of success in organized crime in Tucson. However, it was a short ladder for Milt became involved in Joe B's attempted takeover of the New York board of directors. The enforcers for the other board members did not take kindly to Milt's cocky attitude and had an up-and-coming member of the crime family for whom he worked assassinate him.

Des Goodlove discovered she had hidden talents for business innovation and efficiency. She operated 10 massage parlors in Tucson and Phoenix and made many politically influential friends by offering them special treatment at the hands (and orifices) of her best girls. She ran for political office and won on a platform to extend Social Security to sex workers, which was very popular. One of her side projects was to collect semen from her clients, refine it, and use it to make a topical ointment for women to use as a skin and hair conditioner. Her facial cream sold for over $100 and was in great demand from Hollywood starlets and those who had such aspirations. They were amazed at the healthy glow bestowed on them by the product.

Des was at work developing ingestible and injectable forms of her products for reducing anxiety, elevating mood, increasing lifespan, and augmenting brain function. She endowed a chair for

Scientific Semen Studies (known by insiders as 3S) at the University of Arizona and funded several long-term research programs. Results of those studies supported the nutritional benefits of her concoctions which were high in zinc, potassium, magnesium, calcium citrate, nerve growth factor, oxytocin, progesterone, estrone, serotonin, and melatonin.

Bud Odette was accepted to graduate school at the University of Arizona and did his dissertation on the syntactic facilitation of verbal learning. One day in Tucson, he and some graduate student friends walked into the Kon Tiki seeking relief from the blistering heat, so hot that they left footprints in the pavement of the parking lot. He thought he saw Milt Grubbs in the dim light, sitting under one of the palm frond canopied tables with some other men, all dressed in suits. My eyes must be deceiving me, he thought. He had never seen Milt in a suit and never knew him to sport a mustache, as this gent did. And he couldn't imagine why he would be in Tucson. He kept sneaking looks at the gentleman but, after a couple of Zombies, he dismissed the idea as being so improbable as to be absurd.

Bud did a clinical internship in California, became a professor in a medical school, wrote many journal articles based on research in Psychological Type, and penned seven books. He was an expert in personality psychology, post-traumatic stress disorder (PTSD), and Family Psychotherapy.

Zack finally found someone who complimented his intuitive feeling orientation, his one true love. They married, and he become serious about his career, completing a course in criminal justice at the University of Minnesota. He went through police training and became a patrolman for the City of Northfield, focusing his efforts on preventing youth from pursuing lives of crime. One of his programs was to establish an annual Snooker and Pool Championship, held at Tiny's pool hall. Tiny provided free lessons for those who wanted to compete on Saturday afternoons throughout the year.

Zack went on to become Chief of Police after he exposed wrong doing, namely the cover-up of the Fat Freddy Ferguson affair, by the previous inhabitant of that office,. Zack instituted reforms in police training to require humane treatment and appropriate disposition of disabled individuals and those going through periods of emotional distress. He was nationally recognized for his efforts in this regard at a time when such procedures were not widely accepted.

After Zack retired from the police force, he continued to participate in public life, being named to the boards of several volunteer organizations and frequently making speeches focused on matters of concern to the citizens of Northfield. He doted on his four grandchildren until he died at age 79 from kidney failure.

Becky married Charley Weldon but they were divorced within 3 months when she discovered that he was being unfaithful. She was unable to control her rage over the humiliation she experienced and obsessed about how to obtain revenge. Eventually, she purchased a derringer and followed him to Dundas Dine and Dance where she shot him in the head while dancing past the table where he sat. She claimed temporary insanity as her defense and spent 10 years confined to the state hospital in Rochester. When she was released, she worked as a waitress and busgirl at the Ideal Cafe and wrote a novel based on her prison experiences. The story was later turned into a TV docudrama that was well received.

ABOUT THE AUTHOR

Gerald D. Otis

Gerald D. Otis is a retired research and clinical psychologist, woodworker, and computer programmer residing in Las Cruces, NM. Dr. Otis writes books about whatever strikes his fancy. His first endeavor, Joseph Lee Heywood: His Life and Tragic Death, is a biography of the heroic bank teller in the author's hometown who was shot dead by the marauding Jesse James Gang in 1876. Serendipity while writing that book led to Paroxysm: Love, Murder, and Justice in Post Civil War Washington, DC, a historical novel about one of the most renowned murder trials of the 19th Century. When an old friend was spirited away to an asylum by unscrupulous authorities, he wrote the exposè Presumed Crazy: A Fisherman Gets Entangled in the Mental Health Gulag. A 50-year follow-up study and analysis of personality and attitudinal characteristics of physicians produced Physician Career Choice and Satisfaction (with Naomi L. Quenk). He is currently working on another novel, based on his work with veterans suffering

from combat-related PTSD.
https://www.amazon.com /~/e/B0055B0G7G